D1064118

ASH ROAD

ash road

By
Ivan Southall

With Drawings by
CLEM SEALE

ANGUS AND ROBERTSON

First Published in 1965 by

ANGUS AND ROBERTSON (PUBLISHERS) PTY LTD

221 George Street, Sydney
54 Bartholomew Close, London
107 Elizabeth Street, Melbourne
65 High Street, Singapore

Reprinted 1966 (twice), 1967, 1969, 1971

The Children's Book Council of Australia
BOOK OF THE YEAR, 1966

National Library of Australia
card number and ISBN 0 207 94629 9

PRINTED IN HONG KONG

CONTENTS

For years I lived on a long hill on a winding country road. It wasn't called Ash Road—or was it, I wonder? For all I know, it could have been called by that name once.

All the people who lived on that road I called my friends, and I still do; but I have peopled the Ash Road of this story with men and women and boys and girls who live on it only in my imagination. They are real in the sense that every character in a story must grow out of people the author knows or out of himself, but none of them is intended to represent an actual person.

Even Lorna—to whose memory I dedicate *Ash Road* with love —was another Lorna, a Lorna I knew first in my childhood and lost only a short time ago.

But the event upon which the story is based is not invented. When it started we all knew it had started, and when it ended we could not believe it.

I.S.

1. The North Wind

ON Friday, 12th January, in the late afternoon, the three boys camped in the scrub about a mile from Tinley. It wasn't the best spot to pick but at least there was water; and they were very tired.

They had escaped from the city for a glorious week of freedom in the bush. They had never done it before. They had planned it for months. At first their parents had said no, firmly no, but the boys had nagged and nagged. At last they had hit upon the ruse of encouraging the idea that Harry's parents would agree if Graham's parents would agree if Wallace's parents would agree. In the long run the ruse had worked. The different parents—who rarely saw one another—were not anxious to be regarded by the others as over-protective. After all, the boys were all soon to be fourth-formers—old enough, surely, to take care of themselves and to keep out of trouble for a few days. Not so many years back boys of that age had been out in the world earning a living.

They caught a morning train to the hills, got out at Barkley station, hitched up their packs, and started walking. They felt marvellous, unrestricted, like young colts bred and raised in the home paddock for whom the gate to wide green pastures had been thrown open for the first time.

They were on their own. No one to say, "Do this", "Do that." No one to say, "Come here", "Go there." They smiled at one another, confidentially, conspiratorially, flushing with elation. They were too excited to speak logically; thoughts raced ahead of their tongues and confused their speech. Harry broke into song and Wallace whooped for the sheer joy of living. They wouldn't have exchanged their week in the bush for two weeks or three at the beach with their families; they wouldn't have wished to be anywhere on earth but where they were, striding up the road from Barkley towards Tinley.

There was a bus to Tinley, but they didn't want to take it. A car stopped and the driver offered them a lift, but they waved him on. They wanted none of the trappings of the adult world. They wanted freedom from home, from reminders of school or study, from the endless round of errand-running, music practice, sisters, lawn-mowing, and hot showers. No dressing up for visitors or for Sunday. No shoe-cleaning or rigorous tooth-brushing after each meal. No going to bed while still wide awake. No getting up while still half-asleep. Graham, who had a flair for that sort of thing, made up a poem about it. It came out of the rhythm of his heels striking the road. For a single glowing moment he saw it as a whole, but when he tried to give voice to it, so that he could share it with Wallace and Harry, he lost it. It was one of those rare moments when all the things of heaven and earth are private and personal property, a moment so rare that it might come to him again only once or twice in his lifetime. It was a feeling, not really a thought, and the poem that belonged to it was never to be spoken or written down; it belonged wholly to the moment and would remain a part of the warm and personal mystery of realizing that he was someone different from everyone else in the world, someone separate from everything and everybody that ever existed. Separate, but not cut off. Separate, but belonging.

The north wind blew, gusting, a hot and oppressive summer wind, and there was not a cloud in the sky, and away to their right were the mountains hazed on the high horizon, not particularly grand and rugged, but a range of old mountains worn smooth, folded by numerous deep gullies, timbered by forests of great eucalypts, peppered with rooftops, slashed by the broad scars of the fire-breaks, surmounted at the highest point by tall steel towers that transmitted television signals to the city on the plain in the west. On the foothills, the soil in places was thin and yellow and the trees were only twenty or thirty feet high. Farther up in the folds of the hills there were trees with enough timber in each of them to build a house; there were ferns three times the height of a man, and springs of clear water, and orchids growing wild and curious fungi and thousands of birds and tiny creatures and vegetation so dense that neither man nor boy could push through it. There were gentle slopes and saddles between the hills and other slopes that went up at very steep angles for a thousand feet or more. There were pockets of unspoiled country, wild, uninhabitable, where a boy could be king of the earth.

Perhaps this last thought had not occurred to Graham before. He had never really expected his parents to give way. His parents were straight-laced people, extremely old-fashioned about some things. Wallace might have been allowed to grow his hair a little longer than usual, Harry might have been able to wear casual clothes a little more "extreme" than usual, but not Graham. Graham had to be respectable, neat and tidy, an example. He wearied terribly of having to be an example, because he was sure he wasn't one at all. No one took any notice of him. In his own opinion he was a nobody. He often wondered why Wallace and Harry accepted him, but he didn't wonder too deeply, in case he broke the spell and they stopped being friendly to him. It was good being near Wallace, because Wallace was a big chap, burly, almost as rugged as a man; a strong character, Graham thought. Harry, on the other hand, was clever, but no one sneered at Harry's cleverness, because he was also the best runner for his age in the school. Graham was neither burly nor clever. All he had was sensibility, a feeling for other people, an unusual gentleness for his fifteen years, though he tried very hard to hide it. He often spoke roughly and laughed loudly so that others would think he was manly. And they did think it, too, when they bothered to notice him at all; they thought he was loyal and dependable and sensible. They weren't completely wrong.

The boys walked on along the road to Tinley in the blistering heat of the sun, and their packs became heavier and their pace slower. Sometimes they sat in the shade to cool off and to ease their shoulders. More cars stopped to offer them a lift, but each of them they waved on. They were on their own. They wanted no one.

For their lunch they dug a shallow hole and gathered sticks and made a small fire at the roadside to grill their sausages and boil water for instant coffee. Coffee, they felt, good and strong, was the sort of drink a fellow would have when he lived on his own, when he was a man. The water hadn't even started bubbling in the billy-can, the sausages were not even spitting, when a car pulled up and a woman called to them: "Put that fire out!"

The boys stared at her. She looked like an angry schoolmistress. "You heard me," she said. "Put it out."

"We're only havin' our lunch, lady," said Wallace. "What's wrong with that?"

"You boys are old enough to know better. Put it out at once or I'll report you to the police. There's a £200 fine and a jail sentence for lighting a fire in the open on a day like this."

"Crikey, it's only a little fire," complained Wallace. "We've dug a hole an' all. We're watchin' it."

"Put it out quickly. Tip your water over it."

"Fair go, lady," said Wallace. "What are we supposed to drink? It's a hot day."

It was Harry who lifted the billy off with a stick and emptied the water into the hole, for he had suddenly become aware of the heat and the strength of the north wind, of the way it fanned the flames, of the way the smoke scattered.

"Now stamp on it," the woman called. "Get it out. The last spark. Put it all out."

She watched them with a set face until they had done it; then she said, "If you want hot water on a day like this, go into a house somewhere and ask for it nicely. Fire is a dangerous plaything at this time of year. Don't forget it."

She drove on, and the boys were left looking at one another glumly. "Plaything, my fat aunt," said Wallace.

"Wouldn't it make you sick?" snorted Graham.

"I suppose she was right, though," said Harry.

"We were watchin' it. It couldn't have done any harm." Wallace was very upset. "If we can't light a fire, what are we goin' to eat and drink? What about our sausages an' all?"

"I don't know," said Graham.

"It's *stupid*. All right for her. She can go home and switch on the stove. Grown-ups. You can't get away from them. Two-hundred pound fine for cookin' your lunch! Go to jail for drinkin' coffee! I suppose we're expected to starve to death."

"We've got some buns," said Harry.

"Buns!"

"And we can drink water."

"Whose side are you on? I want *coffee* and *sausages*."

Another car heading in the opposite direction pulled up. It was a utility truck, and at the wheel was a man who looked like a farmer. "You boys aren't lighting a fire, are you?" he said.

"No," said Wallace sullenly.

"Make sure you don't."

They had buns for lunch, and water. Much of the magic of the day had already gone sour on them.

There had been a time, not so long ago, when people went to Tinley for holidays, but the rapid growth of the city had robbed the place of its few modest charms and its isolation. From a quiet little township in the western foothills of the ranges, it had become a straggling and untidy outer suburb of unmade streets and low-cost houses. Speculators had put up signs everywhere (*Choice Home Sites, Elevated Building Blocks, Land on £5 Deposit*). Surveyors had marked the bush with a maze of blazed trees and little white pegs hard-driven into the hungry yellow earth to define new roads and lot numbers. Here and there in the middle of it all, in the dusty wilderness, a few timber-framed houses had taken shape or were partly built.

It was scrubby country, rocky, and the indigenous trees were not tall and straight-grained but twisted and stunted and tough.

It was brittle country. The grasses were sharp and wiry, and the tangled growth fostered by the warm spring rains was by mid-January a fire-trap, a fuse waiting to be lit by a spark or a flash of lightning. The bush behind Tinley as far as the lower slopes of the ranges was a gigantic bomb set to explode.

It had been like that around Tinley almost every January for generations, and for generations men had treated this country with the utmost respect. Only once had it got away. That was back in 1913. The forests had dissolved in fire. Pillars and sheets of flame had swept into the ranges, up through the folds, along the saddles, over the top, and down the other side. Scores of houses had vanished from the earth. Tens of thousands of acres of forest had been stripped bare. Fourteen people had died.

So now no tractor drove without a spark arrester, no householder dared burn rubbish out of doors, no one threw a match away until it was cold and black, smokers deliberately screwed their cigarette stubs into the dust, no one dropped broken glass or bottles that might by chance concentrate the sun's rays on to an inflammable substance, every wisp of smoke and every glimmer of flame seen by day or by night had to be accounted for and accounted for quickly. When the north wind blew there was not a second to lose, for in midsummer the north wind came hot and hard and fiercely dry. Behind its every gust lay two thousand miles of the continental land mass, a land mass baked brown and crisp by the burning sun. The north wind itself was like fire without the flame.

Soon enough the resentment eased out of the boys. They were too young and too free at heart to be miserable for long. Each had several pounds in his pocket (saved over a period of months), and they felt like millionaires. When they got to Tinley they bought pies and cokes and ice creams to fill up on and more buns and more sausages to take away with them, and for a few shillings a tiny heater, no larger than a shoe-polish tin, that burned methylated spirits with a hot blue flame and no smoke. "Works just like a gas stove," the man in the shop said. "Clear the ground, scoop out a hole, put some stones around it to break the wind and it'll be as safe as houses."

They hadn't gone much more than a mile beyond Tinley towards the ranges when Wallace said, "I'm dog-tired. Let's find a creek or somethin' and camp."

"Good idea," said Graham, thankfully, for he would never have suggested it himself.

They fried sausages and made coffee, and talked, and swatted at mosquitoes, and watched the stars come out, and listened to the hot dry wind creaking and crackling through the trees. Then they shone their torches into the undergrowth and up over their heads through the foliage. Insects glowed and flickered in the beams. "Light bends, you know," said Harry, waving his torch from side to side. "But it won't bend for me."

They hadn't bothered to put the tent up; they wriggled into their sleeping-bags in the open.

"Hope it doesn't rain," said Graham.

Listening to voices, even one's own, was sort of nice in the dark.

"My dad says it won't rain for a month." (That came from Harry.)

"Hot, isn't it?" (Graham again, though that one or another should say it was not important. That the words should keep going was the thing.)

"Stinkin' hot," agreed Wallace.

"These sleeping-bags'll be like ovens before long."

"Better than bein' eaten by the mozzies."

"I've got some repellent if you want it."

"Beaut, isn't it, bein' on our own."

"Super."

"Makes you feel good. I don't mean goodie-goodie. You know, *good*."

"Tough?"

"Yeh. In a way."

"Better chuck us that repellent."

"Makes you feel as though you'd like to do something you've never done before?"

"Like what?"

"I don't know. Like somethin' different. Like somethin' that'd get your name in the papers."

"Like making a parachute jump?"

"Yeh. That's what I mean. Like driving a car or chopping down a tree or having a shave, maybe."

"I shave once a week. Every Wednesday."

"Honest?"

"With dad's shaver. Electric razors are beaut. Much better than blades."

"Gee."

"I reckon they give you a cleaner shave."

"My dad says they're useless. Wouldn't shave a baby, he says."

"He can't use 'em right. They shave me good."

"I wonder what it's like makin' a parachute jump?"

They heard cars on the main road in the distance, and a dog barking somewhere.

"What'll we do tomorrow?"

"Find a better spot than this and get organized."

"Don't want to get too far from Tinley."

"Yeh. We've got to go in for grub, you know."

"Two or three miles out, I reckon. We don't want the local kids finding out where we are."

"No fear. They'd be raidin' us an' all."

"When'll we start out for the Pinkards' place?"

"I dunno. I dunno that I want to go much. It's a heck of a long way from here and if his mum and dad are there it'll spoil the fun a bit."

"Well, we said we'd go, didn't we? And I reckon it'd be good. All those cattle and everything."

"Yeh. If there *are* any cattle. You can never believe a word Jerry Pinkard says. He's such a bloomin' show-off."

"Crikey. Jerry wouldn't lie about that. You've seen the photographs. He couldn't fake the photographs."

"Wouldn't put it past him. What do you reckon, Harry?"

"Well, I'd like to see the place. And I don't reckon he would have asked us if it wasn't fair dinkum. I'd say start heading his way about Wednesday or Thursday. No good getting there any sooner because they won't be there."

"Did you find Ash Road on the map?"

"Yeh. It's there all right. I reckon it'll take us about a day."

They heard a bough crack from a tree and fall.

"Crikey," said Wallace, "the wind's strong."

"We'd look good if one of those landed on top of us."

"Not scared, are you?"

"Huh. Come off it."

They heard frogs and crickets and leaves and snapping twigs and big moth wings.

"Who wants a cigarette?"

"Eh?"

"You heard."

"You didn't bring them, did you?" said Harry. "Not after everything they said."

"Couldn't throw 'em away," said Wallace. "Now could I?"

"You know we promised."

"Yeh, yeh. I know. Do you want one?"

"I promised not to," said Harry, "and they're bound to ask me."

They heard a screech owl. It sounded like someone being thrown from the top of a cliff.

"I wish we'd brought a lamp," said Wallace.

"I reckon we've got too much already," said Harry. "Any more and we'd need a pack-horse. My shoulders are aching and aching. What do you want a lamp for, anyway?"

"Well, we can't have a camp fire."

"Who wants a camp fire? I wish you'd shut up and let a fella sleep."

"Graham's asleep now, I think."

"Trust Graham. He'd sleep standing up, I reckon."

"Horses sleep standin' up."

"You don't say?"

"Yeh. I saw it on TV."

They heard other sounds. Rustlings, faint cheepings, scratchings.

"Want a cup of coffee?"

"*Another* one?"

"I reckon coffee's great," said Wallace. "They won't give it to me at home."

"Aw, go to sleep."

There was a long pause.

"Gee, it's great, isn't it", said Wallace, "bein' on our own?"
There was no answer.

Wallace was half-awake, half-asleep. He had been asleep for a while, but had become partly aware of his surroundings again, of the wind and the heat. He was wet with perspiration. Graham had been right about sleeping-bags and ovens. Wallace felt that he was being cooked, and his right hip was bruised and sore. He had dug a little hole for his hip, but he must have turned away from it. The trouble was, he couldn't completely wake up. He was in a sort of limbo of acute discomfort but was too hazy in the head to do anything about it.

When at last he managed to open his eyes he became aware of a faint glow. He thought he could smell methylated spirits. He even thought he could see Graham.

"Is that you?" he said.

"Yes," said Graham.

"What are you doin'?"

"Making coffee."

Wallace sat up, panting. He felt giddy. "What are you makin' coffee for?"

"I'm thirsty. Do you want a cup?"

"What's the time?"

"Twenty past one."

"Yeh. I'll have a cup."

Wallace peeled his sleeping-bag down to the waist, and felt better. "Twenty past one!"

"About that."

"Harry's sleepin' all right."

"Trust Harry," said Graham. "He could sleep anywhere."

Wallace thought he had heard something like that before, but couldn't remember when. "Funny in the bush at night, isn't it? Awful dark."

"Noisy, too. I heard a tree fall down. Not far away either. Woke me up."

"It's the wind."

"Guess so."

"Stinkin' hot, isn't it?"

"You can say that again. But this water's awful slow coming to the boil."

"The wind, I suppose."

"It's taken two lots of metho already," said Graham.

"Have you got the lid on?"

"Can't see when it boils if you've got the lid on."

"Put the lid on, I reckon, or it'll never boil."

"Don't know where the lid is, do you?"

"*Feel* for it. It's there somewhere. Use your torch."

"The battery's flat. Blooming thing. Must have been a crook battery. Hardly used it at all. *Now* look what I've done! There's the metho bottle knocked for six."

"You dope," cried Wallace. "Pick it up quick. Or we'll lose it all."

"The cork's in it." Graham groped for it, feeling a bit of a fool, and said, "Crumbs."

"Now what?"

"The cork's *not* in it, that's what. It must have come out."

"How could it come out? Honest to goodness—"

"It's *burning*," howled Graham.

A blue flame snaked from the little heater up through the rocks towards the bottle in the boy's hand; or at least that was how it seemed to happen. It happened so swiftly it may have deceived the eye. Instinctively, to protect himself, Graham threw the bottle away. There was a shower of fire from its neck, as from the nozzle of a hose.

"Oh my gosh," yelled Wallace and tore off his sleeping-bag. "Harry!" he screamed. "Wake up, Harry!"

They tried to stamp on the fire, but their feet were bare and they couldn't find their shoes. They tried to smother it with their sleeping-bags, but *it* seemed to be everywhere. Harry couldn't even escape from his bag; he couldn't find the zip fastener, and for a few awful moments in his confusion between sleep and wakefulness he thought he was in his bed at home and the house had burst into flames around him. He couldn't come to grips with the situation; he knew only dismay and the wildest kind of alarm. Graham and Wallace, panicking, were throwing themselves from place to place, almost sobbing, beating futilely at a widening arc of fire. Every desperate blow they made seemed to fan the fire, to scatter it farther, to feed it.

"Put it out," shouted Graham. "Put it out."

It wasn't dark any longer. It was a flickering world of tree trunks and twisted boughs, of scrub and saplings and stones, of shouts and wind and smoke and frantic fear. It was so quick. It was terrible.

"Put it out," cried Graham, and Harry fought out of his sleeping-bag, knowing somehow that they'd never get it out by beating at it, that they'd have to get water up from the creek. But all they had was a four-pint billy-can.

The fire was getting away from them in all directions, crackling through the scrub down-wind, burning fiercely back into the wind. Even the ground was burning; grass, roots, and fallen leaves were burning, humus was burning. There were flames on the trees, bark was burning, foliage was flaring, flaring like a whip-crack; and the heat was savage and searing and awful to breathe.

"We can't, we can't," cried Wallace. "What are we going to do?"

They beat at it and beat at it and beat at it.

"Oh gee," sobbed Graham. He was crying, and he hadn't cried since he was twelve years old. "What have I done? *We've got to get it out!*"

Harry was scrambling around wildly, bundling all their things together. It was not that he was more level-headed than the others; it was just that he could see the end more clearly, the hopelessness of it, the absolute certainty of it, the imminent danger of encirclement, the possibility that they might be burnt alive. He could see all this because he hadn't been in it at the start. He wasn't responsible; he hadn't done it; and now that he was wide awake he could see it more clearly. He screamed at them: "Grab your stuff and run for it." But they didn't hear him or didn't want to hear him. They were blackened, their feet were cut, even their hair was singed. They beat and beat, and fire was leaping into the tree tops, and there were no black shadows left, only bright light, red light, yellow light, light that was hard and cruel and terrifying, and there was a rushing sound, a roaring sound, explosions, and smoke, smoke like a hot red fog.

"No," cried Graham. "No, no, no." His arms dropped to his sides and he shook with sobs and Wallace dragged him away. "Oh, Wally," he sobbed. "What have I done?"

"We've got to get out of here," shouted Harry. "Grab the things and run."

"Our shoes?" cried Wallace. "Where are they?"

"I don't know. I don't know."

"We've got to find our shoes."

"They'll kill us," sobbed Graham. "They'll kill us. It's a terrible thing, an awful thing to have done."

"Where'd we put our shoes?" Wallace was running around in circles, blindly. He didn't really know what he was doing. Everything had happened so quickly, so suddenly.

"For Pete's sake run!" shouted Harry.

Something in his voice seemed to get through to Wallace and Graham, and they ran, the three of them, like frightened rabbits. They ran this way and that, hugging their packs and their scorched sleeping-bags, blundering into the scrub, even into the trunks of trees. Fire and confusion seemed to be all around them. The fire's rays darted through the bush; it was like an endless chain with a will of its own, encircling and entangling them, or like a wall that leapt out of the earth to block every fresh run they made for safety. Even the creek couldn't help them. They didn't know where it was. There might as well not have been a creek at all.

"This way," shouted Harry. "A track."

They stumbled back down the track towards Tinley; at least they thought it was towards Tinley, they didn't really know. Perhaps they were running to save their lives, running simply from fear, running away from what they had done.

When they thought they were safe they hid in the bush close to a partly constructed house. They could hear sirens wailing; lights were coming on here and there; the headlamps of cars were beaming and sweeping around curves in the track. They could hear shouts on the wind, they heard a woman cry hysterically, they heard Graham sobbing.

Over all was a red glow.

2. Ash Road

TINLEY was in the foothills near the north-west extremity of the ranges; Ash Road, where the Pinkards had their country place, was in the Prescott district at the head of an immense valley on the opposite side of the ranges, the eastern side and somewhere near the centre, the side that caught the first rays of the rising sun. By car it was about fourteen miles from Tinley to Ash Road; across the ranges in a straight line it was no more than six or seven.

Ash Road didn't go anywhere in particular. It branched off the highway opposite the water-storage reservoir in Prescott Vale—the Prescott Vale Dam—and ended in the bush about two miles farther east. That was the way Ash Road was on the fierce morning of Saturday, 13th January. That was the way it had been, more or less, for a very long time.

The dam hadn't always been there, nor had many of the other landmarks that had become familiar over the years. Tanner's, the oldest house still standing, had been built soon after the turn of the century. The chestnut trees were at Tanner's — tremendous trees, known for generations to every child in miles. Fairhall's place had gone up about 1919. Hobson had planted his apple orchard in 1925. Collins had established his nursery in 1937, and after the war at different times had come the Robertsons, the Georges, the Pinkards, the Buckinghams. Those families, their homes, their farms, and their children were the landmarks of Ash Road.

It hadn't always been called Ash Road. At the start—no one was sure when— it had been a track to a settler's hut. No one knew the name of the settler any more or where his hut had been. Later it had been used as a road to the gold diggings. Not many people knew of the diggings any more, either. The shafts had caved in or grown over. Old-timers, in their youth, had dropped dead horses down the shafts to spare themselves the effort of digging pits; but now, apart from a pony or two, there wasn't a horse to be found from one end of Ash Road to the other and only one genuine old timer, Grandpa Tanner. Most of the giant mountain ashes had gone, too. A few were left along the roadside, standing here and there among lesser trees, but their days seemed to be numbered. They were a constant danger to power lines and telephone lines, and, had it not been for the unyielding stubbornness and vigilance of the residents of Ash Road, one authority or another would have felled them years ago.

There were several look-outs on the surrounding hills from which one could see down most of the gravelled length of Ash Road. It was predominantly red in colour, with four distinct bends and two steep dips, flanked on either side by a maze of creeks and springs. Oddly enough, the road was at its lowest at the farthermost point from the dam. There it ran out into the unspoiled bush, and there the Pinkards grazed a few cattle on eighty rough acres. (The Pinkards lived in the city and came up sometimes at weekends.) Back towards the dam, where the land improved, a second generation of Hobsons tended the apple orchard and the Georges grew carrots for the city market and berries for the local jam factory. Farther up the long hill, just short of the crossroad that provided the quickest route into Prescott, were the Fairhalls, the Buckinghams, and Grandpa Tanner, in a group. Adjoining Grandpa Tanner's was a thirty-acre potato paddock, curiously contoured, lying fallow. There the brow of the hill subsided sharply into the source of a spring. On flatter land, still closer to the dam, were about two hundred acres of scrub and timber out of which the nurserymen, James

Collins and Sons, cut new ground year by year as their business
grew. They owned land on both sides of the road. The
Robertsons had a ten-acre corner opposite the dam with their
main frontage to the highway. The highway skirted the dam
for about eight miles. Bill Robertson was a fuel merchant. He
had an agency for petroleum products and a contract for the
supply of firewood to a number of suburban depots.

That was all there was to Ash Road; except that at daybreak
on the morning of Saturday, 13th January, it lay only six and a
half miles across country from Tinley, a fact of which its
residents were strangely unaware. The roads through the hills
wound so much, changed direction so often, that Tinley seemed
to belong to another world. The Ash Road people never thought
of its lying more or less just over the hill, separated from them
by an almost unbroken expanse of forest. They thought of it—
if they thought of it at all—as an oddly inaccessible and un-
interesting place at the end of a long road that they might
travel over once or twice in a lifetime. In fact there were
children on Ash Road who knew nothing of Tinley, had never
heard mention of its name.

Julie Buckingham, who was five years of age, opened to the sun
like a flower. When the morning sun came strongly through her
curtains she stirred; her limbs uncoiled like petals to the light
of day.

It was terribly hot in her room and though she was too young
to worry much about weather—was indeed to a great extent
oblivious of its extremes—she knew that she was very uncomfortable and very thirsty. She padded to the bathroom because it
was easier to reach the taps over the bath than the taps over the
kitchen sink. She turned the tap on, but couldn't turn it off
again. Even Stevie, who was nine, had trouble with it sometimes.

Julie was a bright girl, and usually made the best of things,
even things that grown-ups sometimes got excited about: things
like wet hair or pyjama coats all dripping with bath water. She
was wet, so what did it matter if she put the plug in the bath
and sailed her plastic boat up and down?

When the water came over the top of the bath, she ran to

her parents' bedroom at the front of the house and told her
father. He didn't seem to hear. He made a sound like a grunt
or a groan, but didn't wake up. Then she told her mother, but
her mother merely moaned and didn't wake up either. Then
Julie went to Pippa's bedroom, and from the depths of restless
and perspiring sleep Pippa said: "Go away, nuisance." By this
time water was flowing out of the bathroom doorway and down
the passage.

Julie knew that that was very naughty. The last time it had
happened she had been given a smack on her hand that had
stung, even though she had said it hadn't. Water was a sort of
mystery in her house. At times it didn't seem to matter how
much was used or wasted; at others Mummy and Daddy were
very stern about it and Daddy often tapped the tanks outside
and listened to the sound they made. Sometimes he pulled a
funny face and said: "If it doesn't rain soon we'll be in trouble."

Julie didn't want another smack on her hand, so she crept
out the back door and hid behind the woodshed. After a while,
because nothing had happened, she went back to the house, but
when she saw water dripping down the steps she started crying
just as if she had already been smacked. Then she ran down the
hill and hid in the bush behind the raspberry patch. From there
she could see Grandpa Tanner's house. She loved Grandpa
Tanner. He gave her silver pennies to buy ice-creams with, and
sometimes when he came over for dinner he brought a bag of
sweeties. She could see Grandpa standing outside in his pyjamas.

It was early for Grandpa Tanner to be out of bed. There had
been a time when he had been up around dawn almost every
day, but there was no need for that now. His family had long
since grown up and gone away; his wife Marjorie had been
dead for so many years; the relentless bush had reclaimed his
once splendid farm; dogwood scrub and blackberries had
choked his fruit trees; sorrel and couch grass had overrun his
garden; there was no cow to milk or hens to feed. The milkman
called these days and Grandpa Tanner bought his eggs at the
grocer's shop. There was not much left for Grandpa, really,
except the routine of getting up and of going to bed, and
remembering. Without the Buckinghams life would have been

pretty drab. The Buckingham children meant much more to him than he would have cared to tell anyone, even the Buckinghams.

He was up early because the heat was stifling, and the sun was already glaring, and the north-west wind that had blown all night was still searing the leaves off the trees as it had seared them the day before. Grandpa hated the north wind. He had hated it all his life. It was an evil wind, a wind that angered men and dismayed women and frightened small children. The long grass growing up to the house was as dry as straw, and dust was in the air, and the smell of smoke. It was the smell of smoke more than anything that had got Grandpa out of bed and out of doors in his pyjamas.

He could see no smoke in the sky, but it was in his nostrils, teasing them, and in his mind, in a way, prompting his memory back down the years to that one desperate hour when he had faced an inferno on his own and fought it on his own and beaten it on his own. He had prayed hard at the time, prayed for a wind-change, for rain, for an army of men with beaters; but none of these had come, and he had done it on his own, and had stood blackened and burnt and bare-headed in the paddock, in the prime of his strength, shaking his fist at the heavens.

An old bushman like Grandpa could smell eucalyptus smoke on the wind from a fire burning fifteen or twenty miles away; he could smell it and feel it and see it with his eyes shut, with tingling senses, with an awareness that was electric. He stood almost motionless, every part of him tuned to that faint signal of smoke.

There *was* a fire; it was burning somewhere, and the world around him was set to ignite. It always happened on a day like this; when the north wind raged, the temperature soared, and the hills were so dry that they crackled. Fire at most seasons of the year was nothing but a flame that water could extinguish; in this season, on a day like this, a little flame could in an instant become a monster.

Not in years had Grandpa seen real smoke—the savage, boiling, black-red smoke of a forest fire on the rampage. He had seen the smoke of scrub fires that had got a little out of hand for an hour or two; the smoke when farmers burnt off new ground, or when shire-workers burnt off the roadsides; and the smoke when fire brigades were cleaning up hazardous pockets of bush before the full heat of summer (the boys of the fire brigades enjoyed a good blaze now and then). But he hadn't seen real smoke close to home since 1913. He had read of bad fires and seen far-off glows in the sky by night, particularly in 1939, but those days seemed to have gone; there were too many people now.

Though the presence of fire always tightened him up, Grandpa had never been unduly afraid of it. He knew that fires, unlike earthquakes or avalanches or erupting volcanoes, could be stopped or turned. Men who knew what they were doing could even fight fire with fire. That was what Grandpa had done in 1913, and he had saved his farm though others not so far away had been wiped out. Even the township of Prescott had gone on that day, 13th January. It had been there in the morning, and in the afternoon it was a heap of charred rubbish and the Gibson family had been burnt to death.

That dreadful day had started like this one, even to the day of the month—the same searing northerly, the same faint smell of smoke, the same sort of temperature that had climbed and climbed to over 112 degrees in the shade. And when the fire had come over the top of the range and thundered into the valley like a thousand locomotives steaming abreast, it had become still hotter and hotter—so hot that birds on the wing fell dead and grass started burning almost of its own accord and locked-up houses exploded and creeks boiled.

But that had been a long time ago. It couldn't happen now. Now there were hundreds of fire-fighters trained and equipped at immense expense with fast vehicles and water-tankers and high-pressure hoses. Those boys made fast work of the job; they knew what they were about. Now there were firebreaks through the eucalyptus forests and the pine plantations, great barren scars across the hills with every blade of grass ploughed in, bare earth that could not burn. Now there were many farms, many houses, and most of the old forest areas, the fire-traps, had vanished (that was what everyone said, anyway). Now there were water-towers on the high peaks and in the west of the valley the Prescott Vale Dam, eight miles long and more than half a mile wide. What fire coming down out of the plantations and the forests could consume millions of tons of water? What fire could leap a dam half a mile wide?

Probably the smoke Grandpa could sense wasn't bushfire smoke at all. He couldn't hear sirens and he was sure none had sounded during the night. Except for the blustering wind the valley seemed still to be sleeping. Or perhaps the Fairhalls, across the road—early risers for the past forty years or so—were burning leafy wood in their kitchen stove.

One of the Fairhalls was up. It was Peter, but he wasn't anywhere near the kitchen stove. He was swimming in the creek where Gramps in his younger days had dammed the gully with rocks and mud and the trunks of tree-ferns. But Gramps had not intended it for swimming in. Swimming in creeks was not wise. There were always snakes near water, and there were often snags under the water.

Peter was the only grandson of the Fairhalls, only child of the only son the Fairhalls had, and no one was more conscious of this than Peter himself. It was hard for Peter, for almost all the thoughts and all the love and all the hopes of the whole family were centred upon him. It was a great weight that bowed him down. Everyone was afraid, almost all the time, that something would happen to Peter, that he would be killed in a road accident, or be drowned, or sicken and die.

"Do be careful, Peter." "Take care, Peter." "Watch the road, Peter." "Are you well, Peter?" "Out of those wet clothes, Peter." "I'll rub your chest, Peter." "The doctor's coming, Peter."

He knew what it was all about. He knew that only rarely was their love for him a happy thing; usually it plunged him into a misery of fear. It was like that with both his parents and his grandparents. He sometimes wondered whether his father had grown up the same way, in a state of constant anxiety.

For all that, Peter at thirteen years of age was a healthy lad, even if stubbornly thin. For as far back as he could remember, two weeks of every January—the second and third weeks—had been spent with his grandparents, and almost always Gran had greeted him with the words, "We'll fatten you up in no time at all." Gran and Gramps were unchanging. They always looked the same, always said the same things, always stifled him with their love unless by one deception or another he managed to elude them for a few hours. They never guessed that for years he had swum in the creek in the early morning when the weather was hot. It had to be hot, of course, because even in midsummer creek water was very cold. It brought him out in goose pimples all over, but he loved it; he loved the shock of plunging into it. It was like breaking out of prison.

The creek was his own private secret, because if the news got around it would be the end of it. He told no one about it, not even Pippa Buckingham. Sometimes he felt mean about that, because Pippa was different from everybody else; quite different from other girls, and nothing like a boy. Pippa was a very special sort of person. She always had been as far as Peter was concerned and perhaps she always would be. Peter felt sad when he thought of her. What would he do with himself for a whole week after Pippa had gone on her holidays?

Pippa stirred uneasily. Oddly enough, she knew she was asleep. She could see herself in bed with the bedclothes as usual in complete disorder; with the pillow as usual on the floor; with one arm as usual flopping limply over the edge of the bed. Pippa also knew that it was important that she should wake up, that if she didn't the house would drift out to sea. The house should have been tied up to the pier, but Julie had untied the rope and couldn't tie it up again.

Pippa felt dizzy and hot and bone-weary, unable to pull herself together. After a while she realized that she was sitting up in bed and that the hands of the little clock on her dressing-table showed twenty minutes past five. Her mouth was dry and there was a dull ache in her head. She felt as if she had been baked in an oven. Yet, strangely, she could hear water. It sounded like the bubbling of a mountain stream. Then Julie's voice came back to her from far away: "Pippa, Pippa, I can't turn the tap off."

Pippa stumbled from her bed. The carpet was wet and made a squelching sound under her feet. "Oh," she cried. "Mum! Dad!"

She floundered into the passage. Water was everywhere. She could hear it pouring from the bath onto the floor, and she could see it coursing down the passage into her own room, into Stevie's room, even into the kitchen.

"Oh golly . . . . Dad," she shouted. "Dad!"

She turned the tap off over the bath and stood helplessly, with water over her toes, wondering what to do. She felt limp and useless and completely disheartened. It seemed that the whole day was ruined, that it was all part of a plot to prevent them from leaving on time for their holidays at the beach. She heard the voices of her mother and father and Stevie calling from his bedroom, "What's the matter?"

"Water," she cried. "Water everywhere."

Her father poked his head in through the bathroom door. He looked unshaven and tired. "Godfathers," he said. "Whose work is this?"

"Julie's, I guess," sighed Pippa.

"The little devil. I'll skin her. Bet your life as soon as you're short of water something like this'll happen." He looked around the flooded room and scratched his head. "We can't go away and leave the tanks empty. Not at this time of the year."

Pippa wilted further. This was a complication she hadn't thought of. "Golly," she said, "I hope it doesn't mean we've got to cart well water from Grandpa Tanner's again, in buckets, like last year."

"Of that, young lady, there's every possibility."

The carting had been dreadful. Trudging up and down the hill with buckets was such hard work, such drudgery, and it took so long. Pippa felt absolutely miserable. "Well, I guess I'd better not pull the plug out of the bath?"

"That's right," her father said. "Every drop wasted is another drop to be carted. Throw me the towels. We'd better start mopping it up."

Mrs Buckingham, in the background, was mourning for her carpets. "We'll have to get them outside. I hope they don't take too long to dry. Thank heaven it's a hot day. That's the only good thing you can say for it. Isn't it a *pest?*"

"It's a confounded nuisance," agreed Mr Buckingham. It was rather too early in the morning—that morning in particular

—for anyone to take the incident lightly. "I don't know. Maybe I can put creek water into the tanks, if the blessed pump will work for me. Fool of a thing it is . . . . Where's Julie? *Julie!*"

Stevie came out of his room, rubbing his eyes and stepping gingerly. "What's up?" he said. "What's all the water? Is it raining or something?"

"Stevie," said his mother, "call Julie, will you. I suppose she's outside somewhere. And bring a couple of buckets back with you. Oh, isn't it a crying shame. And it's *so* hot. I just don't feel up to dealing with a mess like this."

"Little devil," snapped Mr Buckingham. "Been sailing boats on it, too. She'll have to have a jolly good smack this time."

"She did tell me," said Pippa, "but I thought I was dreaming."

"She *told* you! And you did nothing about it? Really, lass!"

"I wasn't awake, Dad . . . I didn't . . ."

Stevie came back with the buckets. He was still half asleep. "Can't find Julie," he said. "She doesn't answer."

"She'll be hiding somewhere. Put your shoes on, lad. Go look for her. She won't be far. She knows she's done wrong all right. Little devil."

"Dad," said Stevie vaguely, "I reckon I smell smoke."

"Smoke? What sort of smoke?"

"I don't know."

"You've got a job to do, Stevie," said Mrs Buckingham. "Find Julie. Now get yourself dressed and do it. And you'd better help him, Pippa."

"Funny, that," said Mr Buckingham. "I had an idea I could smell smoke myself. You couldn't see it, lad?"

Stevie shook his head.

"I think I can smell it, too," said Pippa. "Like when the fire brigade burnt off the Georges' bit of bush last year."

There was silence for a moment; all four of them, man and boy, woman and girl, stood in water, tensely, each reluctant to take the conversation any further, Stevie because he wasn't sure what it was all about, anyway. There was something of the ostrich in each of them; what they didn't face they didn't have to worry about.

"We'd better clean up this mess," said Mrs Buckingham, "or we'll be lucky to get away by noon."

"In a minute, in a minute," her husband said. He squelched to the kitchen and out onto the steps at the back. He was frankly fearful that he might see smoke in the sky, but he didn't. The sky, perhaps, was not as clear as it should have been, but that was probably the wind, probably dust. He could feel the wind on his face, hot and positive, almost like a physical blow, and he could hear it roaring in the tall timber. He looked around, and Pippa was behind him. "If there is a fire, lass," he said, "it must be a long way off. Nothing to worry about, I should think. Bad day, though. A shocker. It's not going to do the berries any good. Finish them off completely. The Georges won't be too happy about it. Wouldn't hurt, you know, to give them a hand for an hour or two. I would if old George wasn't so blamed independent."

The Georges were in the raspberries, in the midst of the long rows that leaned and lurched to the wind, rows already limp from the heat, their leaves already scorched.

All three of the Georges were there—father, son John, and daughter Lorna—streaked with sweat and dust, hands bleeding with the pulp of fruit so soft that it bruised at the lightest touch. They had been there since the first light of day, not from any love of the dawn, but to save what they could of their crop before the sun sucked the juices out of it. But this had happened already, really. It was a poor man's yield, what was left of it, and that was what old man George kept mumbling to himself. A man worked like a slave and what did he get for it? A wind hotter than fire on his neck at five-thirty in the morning, and a whining son with itchy feet, fretting to leap on his motor cycle and roar into town; a whining son more concerned with heroics, with the smell of smoke, than with the sight of raspberries cooking on the canes. The smell of smoke to this young man was like the smell of fox to a hound. It was the call to the hunt.

"Forget the smoke, will you," old man George grated. "If there's a fire, let someone else do the fighting. We've got a big enough fight of our own."

John didn't see it that way. His father's self-interest and self-concern infuriated him. "If there's a fire," he said, "my place is with the boys. It's my duty. I'm their lieutenant. What the devil are they going to think if their lieutenant isn't there?"

"I don't care what they think. Your place is here with me. This farm's your duty. In heat like this you're a farmer first. It's your bread and butter. Fighting fires isn't."

One hundred and one degrees yesterday, ninety-nine the day before, ninety-seven the day before that; too much for raspberries unless they were in the gullies where humus was deep and soils were moist. The Georges' raspberries were in the open, on the hillside, because they had worked the gullies for so long that raspberries wouldn't grow there any more; there was a disease in the soil that stunted their growth. This happened to everyone, but old man George saw it as one more act of fate directed specifically against him. He'd have saved his crop if it had been in the gullies.

"You haven't had a call," he grumbled. "No one's had a call."

"Fat lot of hope I'd have of hearing the phone from here, anyway."

"You'd hear the siren, wouldn't you? And there hasn't been a siren."

"Even that's a toss-up," said John, with an acute sense of guilt. "The way the wind's blowing it'd blow the sound away."

The old man turned on his daughter. "Have you heard sirens, Lorna?"

She hadn't and she had to admit it, even though her sympathies were with her brother.

"There," the old man said. "Her ears are the youngest of the lot of us and she hasn't heard anything. It's heat, that's what, not smoke—sheer blistering heat. Fryin' the sap in the trees."

Lorna felt like saying, "Don't be stupid. Don't act like a stupid old man. Don't make me feel ashamed of you," but she couldn't say it and would never say it. She couldn't hurt her father. He was hurt enough already, for life had hurt him all along the line and Lorna knew all about it. Old man George was born unlucky, unlucky in all things except his children.

John was a fine son, and as for Lorna, how she could be her
mother's daughter, heaven alone knew.

Lorna was capable and level-headed and supremely patient,
and over the summer months this was probably just as well. The
family relied upon her, heavily, for her mother was ill:
emotionally ill, they said. She was a weak woman who couldn't
face up to life. If she had married a banker or a prosperous
storekeeper and lived in comparative ease she might never have
fallen ill at all, but she had married a farmer much older than
herself, a small farmer whose crops were at the mercy of the
elements. They said she would get better, but it would take a
long period of complete rest in a convalescent home. Lorna was
part of the cure, for her mother knew that her husband and
John were secure for as long as she cared to leave them in
Lorna's hands. Indeed she had always relied a great deal on
Lorna; far too much, probably; but she was that kind of
woman. She had never realized that Lorna's childhood had
been something like a sentence to hard labour, hard labour in
the house and hard labour in the paddocks. Old man George
didn't realize it either, but for a completely different reason. To
his mind one's children were duty-bound. Life wasn't a game,
it was a battle, and everyone was in it.

"Old man George is a tyrant," people used to say, "and his
kids can't have much spirit or they'd buck against it." (People
used to wonder in private, though. John's tenacious loyalty to
his father couldn't have been a mark of weakness.) And
Lorna's friends of her own age, her school friends, were not
friends in the proper sense. Most of the time they couldn't be
bothered with her because she was always wanted at home, and
even when she said she'd meet them somewhere she hardly ever
turned up. "Lorna George," they used to say, "she's no fun.
She always lets you down." (Pippa, too, had said it at times,
angrily and irritably, though her anger was not directed against
Lorna as a person; it was directed against something that Lorna
seemed to stand for. Something *un-Australian,* whatever that
might mean.)

It was tough luck for Lorna that school-holiday time was
also berry-picking time. Berries, along with carrots, came before
holidays, before anything. Young carrots were a terrible worry

during December and January; in the course of a single day tender plants could die in their tens of thousands, hot sun and scorching wind could burn them into the ground, and when that happened the Georges were in for a bleak winter, for carrots were the winter crop. Carrots were money during the winter.

Night and day for weeks on end the diesel engine on the creek pumped and the sprinklers turned, protecting the carrots from the malignant heat and wind that seemed to strive to destroy them. Every three hours during the day the sprinklers were shifted, and every three hours during the night. It was an endless, wearying chore which John and his father took turn about. Unless it rained—and it didn't rain often at that time of year—they never had a night of unbroken sleep; and they were up again at dawn anyway, when the heat was really on, picking the ripe red berries before the burning sun withered them or scorched them and rendered them worthless.

It was a frantic season, a frantic struggle. Mr George would not employ pickers to help the family out, and every day the berries kept coming, kept ripening, and the hotter the weather the faster they came, until sometimes, as now, they came all at once. Mr George didn't like pickers, he said, because they trampled his strawberries and rough-handled his raspberries. They did more damage than they were worth. Even more than that, he didn't like paying them. They were a luxury, he said, that he couldn't afford. Perhaps they were; but it all added up to form part of the illness that afflicted Lorna's mother. She hated the physical misery of summer with an evil-tempered hatred. Perhaps the doctors realized that, perhaps they didn't; anyway, they took her away from it and she rested blissfully in her convalescent home while Lorna (at fourteen years and three months) cooked and swept and washed clothes and helped with the picking and snatched at her holidays—an hour here and an hour there—when her father would allow her.

To John it was painfully clear that his kid sister had a colourless life. She was much too patient, much too good-natured. The paddock was no place for a girl of her age at this hour, for a girl who had to look after the house and get the meals and everything else as well. She should still be in bed asleep instead of staining her hands almost indelibly with a lot of useless fruit, smearing dirt and juices and sweat across her face every time she brushed the hair from her eyes.

His father was a stubborn old fool; he'd call black white if it suited him. Any reasonable man would admit that the crop was a write-off and start trying to live with the idea. If Lorna were to achieve anything by being here, all right, let her pick; but this was senseless; no less ridiculous than denying the reality of the smoke in the air. Telephone call or no telephone call, John knew he should be on duty. It was his place on a day like this. It was not as if he lived and worked fifty yards from the first station; he lived and worked three miles out. It was too far in an emergency. The other firefighters would be compelled to go without him. And this would be like a ship putting to sea without a navigator.

"For crying out loud, Dad," he said, "we're wasting our time. What's the use of picking the stuff?"

"You'll pick," the old man said sourly, "until I say not to."

"They'll only knock them back, Dad." John didn't say this just to suit himself. He said it because he knew it was a fact. "By the time the factory truck gets here tonight they won't be worth a cracker."

"Now look! Everyone's berries are the same. The factory's got to take them or go without. If they can't put them in cans they'll jam them."

"They don't make jam out of fruit like this."

"I've seen the fruit they make jam with!"

"Honest, Dad," said Lorna, "it *is* pretty hopeless. You can't pick them. They go to mush."

"Don't you turn against me, too. It's bad enough putting up with him. You know what your mother's illness is costing us. We've *got* to get them off."

"Well I think it's time Mum went into a public ward, like the doctor says, whether she likes it or not. It's not fair on you, Dad."

"I'll decide what's fair and what's not fair, and when I want your opinion, Lorna, I'll ask for it."

It was useless. You couldn't argue with him. It always ended in a row. He always went deathly white, and his worn and weary face frightened her. There was a streak in his nature that wouldn't give in, even though he was so tired deep down that the effort of argument exhausted him. He'd probably kill himself in the end; or drop dead for want of giving in over some issue at a sensible time.

So they went on picking, each keeping pace with the others in adjoining rows. Old man George knew that the fruit was rotten, but a devil in him wouldn't let him stop, kept telling him there was a chance that the factory might not inspect the fruit closely, perhaps until tomorrow, might blame the carrier for bouncing it around too much on the back of the truck, might even accept it despite its condition for any of a dozen reasons. Then he heard the siren.

An urgent, demanding cry it was, wailing through the gullies, fighting to be heard over the buffeting wind. It came faintly at first, then broke over them like a wave. There was no denying it. There was something about a siren that welled up from the inside. It was almost like being sick.

"See you later," said John. It was not an apology or a request for permission to leave; he was running before it was fully out, running up the rows, up the hill, towards the house. His father watched him go, too numb at heart to protest, even to try to call him back. He stood almost still, dripping with perspiration, and his strength seemed to be flowing away through his feet into the ground.

"Lorna," he sighed. "Oh, Lorna . . . ."

He may not have meant it that way, but his manner of utterance committed her. She'd have to stick it out. She'd have to take John's place. She'd have to pick until she fainted from heat or the old man gave in.

3. Fire Warning

PETER FAIRHALL was making his way up from the creek towards his grandparents' house when he heard the siren. He was out in the middle of the paddock, walking carefully between the rows of young gladioli planted by the bulb-grower who rented a few acres of Fairhall land. Peter's grandfather hadn't farmed the place in years.

It was the first time Peter had heard a fire warning in the bush, but he recognized it instantly for what it was and stopped in his stride.

He had sometimes wondered what it would be like to hear the siren when the danger was real, when everything was tinder-dry and the notorious north wind was squarely set to fan an inferno. Now he knew. He felt nothing but unbelief. How could there be a fire? How could it possibly happen? It happened in the newspapers, but not in real life. There was a gap between the page of a newspaper and real life. It wasn't distance; it wasn't time; it was the difference between what happened to other people and what happened to oneself.

But the siren still blew. It swelled and faded and swelled again, and Peter realized that he was faintly unnerved, at a loss, as if suddenly cut off from the normal and unthinking processes that would have continued to impel him up the hill towards the house. He had stopped moving. He had almost stopped breathing.

Fire would be very dangerous on a day like this. There was no sign of fire near by, but perhaps he had been smelling smoke for a while without realizing it. He could see a clear horizon at about five miles in the south and the west, and a hazed horizon of about twenty miles in the east. His eyes spanned that vast arc of country in a few seconds, and there was nothing vaguely like a smoke cloud. Only in the north was his horizon shortened by the brow of the long hill. There could have been a fire in that direction, for the sky there looked different; it was brighter and whiter, and though he avoided the sun there was something odd about it. He sensed that there was a veil across it, like the filmiest of silks or chiffons. And the wailing siren told him what it was.

He shivered. It was a strange feeling, almost like a vision. He saw a horizon of fire and a sky of fire. It was so real that he could almost feel its flashing heat: a wave of heat so fierce that his eyes actually watered. He saw the hills in flames, the trees burning like a forest of gigantic tapers, even though at the same time he saw them as they really were, dusty green and brown, wind-tossed, as he had seen them on rough days in January ever since he could remember. What a stupid thought it was; what a terrible thing to think up; almost like wishing it to happen. But what a sight it would make; what an incredible spectacle it would be: the earth burning, the sky burning, people fleeing. He could see the black figures silhouetted against the flames, running grotesquely with their arms waving over their heads. But now he was separate from it himself; he was seeing it, but he wasn't in it. It was like watching a film on a screen. You knew it wasn't real and the actors couldn't get hurt, even when the fire overtook and overwhelmed them.

But the sound he could hear was the siren still wailing, a sound with a strange ability to drift about in the air; at one moment close and immediate, a few moments later distant and far away; like a ship on a violent sea heaving into sight then vanishing into troughs.

"Peter!"

Perhaps the sound was a trick of the wind, that horrid wind roaring in the timber, blustering against him, raising puffs of dust from every area of dry ground, imposing upon the birds extraordinary patterns of flight, flaking leaves from trees, snapping dead twigs from high branches and throwing them to the earth.

"Peter! Peter, come here!"

He had heard his grandmother's voice the first time, really, but the effort of acknowledging it had been beyond him. He turned and saw her standing near the hen-house. "Coming," he called, though it was the last thing he wanted to do. It was an invasion of his privacy; almost like an interruption in the middle of reading a long-awaited letter. Her demanding voice seemed to have destroyed something.

"Hurry on. Hurry on," she shouted.

"Oh golly," he groaned.

"What is it, Gran?" he called. "What's wrong?"

"Can't you hear the siren? It's a fire. You'll have to go home."

He felt suddenly bereft; something he valued greatly seemed to have been taken from him. "Oh no," he said, "not that. Whatever for?"

A motor cycle howled up the long hill trailing a billow of orange-coloured dust. It flashed past Peter's vision, through the trees, and roared on up the hill and over it. He knew who it was. John George wasn't going home. He was going out to do a job like a man. But of course John *was* a man. He wasn't a molly-coddled kid.

Pippa heard the siren, too. She was down the hill not far from the creek where her father had his pump—the pump that never worked when it was supposed to; only when it didn't matter. It was not the same creek as the Fairhalls'.

Pippa was looking for Julie, and the possibility that Julie might have wandered away and become truly lost had assumed a sudden and grim reality. Until the instant of the siren the thought as such had not occurred to Pippa; after all, when Julie had been naughty she always went to earth, simply froze and remained silent. One could stand and bellow her name half a dozen paces from her and never guess she was there. Julie wouldn't answer until she thought the crisis was past, until the voice that called her began to get tired. Finding Julie when Julie knew she was in disgrace was just about impossible.

For a few moments Pippa was frightened. The bush along the creek was thick and wild and Grandpa Tanner said there were old mine holes in it, though no one had ever come across them. How terrible it would be if Julie really were lost and a fire came. Pippa couldn't suppress a little cry of anguish. She had never thought of anything like that before; but she had never heard a fire warning before, either, on a suffocating midsummer morning like this one. She called Julie's name loudly; at least she intended to call it loudly, but her voice came with a break in it. The only response was a distant wind-blown cry from Stevie: "Gee whiz. Wombat tracks!"

That was Stevie all over. His help was worse than useless. Most of the time he forgot what he was about and started stalking birds or rabbits or turning over stones looking for beetles and shiny black worms with yellow bands on their bodies.

"Stevie," she cried, "can't you hear that siren?"

There was no reply; she couldn't see him; didn't know where he was; she guessed he was already on the trail of the wombat with everything else forgotten. Then she heard him breaking out of the bush surprisingly close to her, and he appeared at the edge of the cleared land in the gully. "Say, Pippa," he yelled. "That's the siren." He stood with legs apart and arms apart as though about to engage an enemy in combat. "The siren," he shrilled. "There's a fire." And he started running up the hill.

"Stevie," Pippa cried, "come back! We've got to find Julie."

"Blow Julie," yelled Stevie—or that was what it sounded like; the roar of wind in the trees didn't make hearing easy. "You find her. I want to see the fire."

She could never stop him. It was a waste of time and breath calling after him. He was off, as fast as he could go, beyond all hope of claiming his attention over the wind.

She was on her own, and the tossing bush was all around her, and the wailing siren seemed to be crying inside her.

"Julie," she screamed suddenly. "Answer me. Where are you, Julie? You won't get smacked, Julie. Answer me, sweetie!"

Stevie pounded up the hill and saw his parents near the apple-tree, Dad in shorts and singlet, Mum in her dressing-gown. Mum looked tall and thin in her dressing-gown, though she wasn't really. She was gripping Dad tightly, almost desperately, by the arm, but Stevie didn't take much notice of that. Mum and Dad were always hanging onto each other as if they were afraid one or the other was going to vanish into thin air. "Gee," Stevie cried breathlessly. "Where is it, Dad?"

They must have heard him, but they ignored him, as they so often did, until he appeared flushed and excited, practically jumping up and down in front of them. "I don't know," his dad said. "Somewhere in the north, I think. Doesn't matter where it is. Anywhere's bad."

Bad? Stevie didn't know what was bad about it. He thought of fires as things the fire-brigades lit, usually in the cool of the evening, and everyone stood and watched the sparks and the flaring foliage and said, "What a sight!"

"Can we go to it, Dad?" Stevie said. "Come on, Dad. Be a sport. Let's go."

His father didn't seem to be listening. Then they heard the motor cycle coming up the road. They heard it howl past with a blare of sound, and Stevie spun away to the side of the house to gasp in admiration at the dust cloud. "Gee whiz," he said, "that's really moving . . . . John's going," he yelled. "Can't we go, too?"

His father was frowning; he seemed agitated. "It's certainly on," he said. "That's John, all right. Of course it *had* to be today."

"The boy'll kill himself if he goes at that pace," said Mrs Buckingham.

"Can we go too, Dad?" shrilled Stevie.

"Be quiet," his mother snapped. "You're not going anywhere. No one's going anywhere."

Mr Buckingham firmly disengaged his wife's clinging hand. "Perhaps I'd better get the car out, at that," he said, "and take a look. Probably only have to drive to the top of the hill. I think we need to know what's going on."

"I don't agree. If you want to find out what's going on, use
the telephone. Ring the brigade. Or ring the Collinses if you
don't want to worry the brigade.'

"The Collinses have been away for a week," he said patiently.
"You know that as well as I do."

"Ring Bill Robertson then. You're always saying he's a
friend of yours. He'll be able to see from there."

"For heaven's sake," said Mr Buckingham, "simmer down,
will you . . . ."

Stevie looked at his mother in surprise. She sounded like a
different person from the mother he knew. "Dad," he said,
"we're going, aren't we? Come on, Dad."

The man seemed to become aware of the boy as the answer
to a problem. "You go yourself, lad. Run to the top of the hill,
and if the smoke looks close get back here at the double. You'll
be back before I'll have time to raise anyone on the phone, anyway. Go on, off with you.

Stevie glanced at his mother and immediately wished he
hadn't, because she said in a tight and strained voice, "I don't
think he should go. I think it's most unwise."

"Oh, for pity's sake," said Mr Buckingham. "Do you think
I'd send the lad if I thought there was any danger? The sky
would be *black* if there was any danger. You're a real panic-
n.erchant, you are. Go on, Stevie; off you run."

Stevie ran. He wanted no more arguments. But his mother's
voice, shrill and strident, pursued him. "What about Julie?
Where's Julie?"

"Julie's all right," he yelled. He didn't mean to speak an
untruth; Julie seemed to belong to another situation, of no
present importance. "Pippa's there."

"What did he say?" the woman said.

Mr Buckingham, still annoyed, hadn't heard Stevie any better
than his wife had. "Oh, she's with Pippa," he grumbled, and
tramped into the house to the telephone. He had forgotten
about the water, of course. It squelched under his feet. "Con-
found it!" he shouted. "What a way to start a holiday! What
a perfect beginning to a hard-earned rest."

Stevie hobbled up the road towards the brow of the long hill.
He couldn't run any more because he had a stitch in his side

and it hurt. He hadn't had a stitch for ages, not since he had
tried to run a quarter of a mile round the Prescott Oval at the
school sports last year. The big boys had done it, so Stevie had
thought he could do it, too.

As he passed the Fairhalls' gate—the Fairhalls' property was
directly opposite his own but the gate wasn't—he wondered
whether Peter knew about the fire. Maybe he ought to run in
and tell Peter—though perhaps it would be best to go on to the
top of the hill first and have a look just to make sure. This was
the exciting sort of news that a fella ought to race with from
house to house, banging on the door, yelling, "Hey, hey, hey.
Have you heard about the fire?" But it was no use going down
the hill and banging on the Georges' door because they knew
already, and it was no use banging on the Hobsons' door because
they were at the beach living in a caravan, and it was no use
going all the way down to Pinkards' because they hardly ever
drove up from town much before eleven o'clock on a Saturday
morning, if they bothered to come at all.

Gee, they were unlucky, all those people, being away. They
wouldn't see the fire. Even the Collinses were away, though
they were different. You could hardly bang on the Collins's
door, because the Collinses were rich and you didn't bang on
rich people's doors. Dad mightn't like it either, because he did
the Collins's books for them every month and Dad said you had
to be polite with clients, but not familiar. If you got too
friendly they might forget to pay you. Dad had been an
accountant for years and years and he said that when people
were short of money it was always their friends that they didn't
pay. Perhaps, Stevie thought, he could bang on the Robertsons'
door; but that was so far he'd be all worn out before he got
there. Gee, running to the Robertsons', opposite the dam, was
even farther than running round the oval.

Bill Robertson, the fuel and oil merchant, could hear the phone
ringing and ringing. He fumbled for his watch under the pillow
and peered at it darkly. It was only twenty to six. At least that
was what it looked like. Or was it half-past eight? No one
would ring him at twenty to six in the morning, so it must have

been half-past eight. He'd slept in. He had a vague idea that he hadn't wanted to sleep in, but couldn't remember why.

He struggled up irritably and sat on the edge of the bed, aching. What a beastly night it had been. In and out of bed three times to the baby, because once his wife closed her eyes it needed a bomb to wake her up. He groped out into the hall and picked up the phone.

"Is that you, Bill?" a voice said.

"Yeh, yeh. Who's that?"

"Don Buckingham."

"Who?"

"Buckingham. Buckingham. Don Buckingham."

"Oh yeh." What in blazes was Buckingham ringing him for? He hardly knew the man. "Yeh," Bill groaned, "what's on your mind?"

"There's a fire warning, Bill. We can't spot it from here. Is it over your way?"

"Fire warning? I didn't hear any siren."

"You wouldn't from there, the way the wind's blowing."

Bill tried to pull himself together. "When was this?"

"Half-past five. A few minutes ago."

"Half-past five!"

"Sorry about this, Bill. It's the wife. You know what women are when there's a bit of smoke about."

"Yeh, yeh, I know. No fire round here, though."

"You're sure, I suppose? You've been outside?"

"Yeh, yeh. No fire round here. See you some time." Bill hung up and leant against the wall. He wasn't surly by nature. It was just that he was exhausted from a stifling and almost sleepless night. Half-past five! The nerve of the fellow, ringing a stranger at that hour. Well, perhaps not a stranger. Buckingham came round once a year at income-tax time to audit the books, but what excuse was that to blow in a man's ear in the middle of the night?

It wasn't night, really. It was broad daylight and wind was slapping against the sun-blinds at the front of the house and banging the loose sheet of iron on the roof of the shed. He opened the front door and squinted into the dazzling light of

the morning. It was cruel. Fire? No sign of fire. Buckingham
had a bee in his bonnet.

He groaned and headed back for bed. He remembered now
why he hadn't wanted to sleep in. There was a drum of diesel
oil to be delivered to the Georges, without fail, first thing,
because old man George said he'd forgotten to reorder and
wouldn't have enough to last out the day. Old liar. He hadn't
reordered because he was too mean to spend his money a
minute before he had to. Old man George was always the same.
Hand to mouth. Not even enough oil up his sleeve to keep his
pump working until Monday. But eight o'clock would be early
enough for old man George, not half-past five.

Back in bed, Bill Robertson started thinking. Perhaps he
should have had a better look. Fire was something not to be
taken too lightly, and after all, Buckingham wasn't a complete
idiot. He'd lived on Ash Road for years, longer than Bill himself, and if anyone's property was inflammable when fire was
around it was Bill's. Buckingham had probably meant well.

He got out of bed again and put on his slippers and dressing-
gown. Then he realized that he was being watched.

"What are you doing up?" his wife said.

He grimaced and went to the door.

Stevie came to the top of the long hill opposite the thirty acres
of fallow ground next to Grandpa Tanner's, not far from the
crossroad that headed out into the bush in one direction and
back into Prescott in the other. This hill was the highest ground,
by a narrow margin, for miles around. In a way it was part of
the chain of mountains that swept across his vision through the
north and the west; perhaps it was the last real foothill in that
section of the Prescott district, for behind Stevie the land slid
down little by little into the main valley between the ranges and
the next mountain chain about twenty miles away.

From the top of the long hill Stevie saw the smoke. It was in
the north, and was like a wide and boiling storm cloud coming
up over the mountains, a big brown cloud torn about at the
edges by the wind; way past the top end of Ash Road where
the Collinses and the Robertsons lived, way past the highway

and the dam, way past places he knew were there but couldn't see, right across on the other side of the ranges.

"Aw gee," he said, "what's the good of that? It's too far away. Now Dad won't take me to see it."

He picked up a stone and threw it at the trunk of a tree. It missed. He was trudging back downhill, dispirited, when he remembered that this was the day for the beach. Mum had said the night before that everyone would have to lend a hand with the packing if they were to get away by ten-thirty and reach the guest house at Deer Sands in good time for lunch. They went to Deer Sands for their holidays every year. Deer Sands was beaut. The thought cheered Stevie no end. His stitch had gone, and he started skipping down the hill.

When he passed the Fairhalls' gate Peter called from the front veranda: "Is that you, Stevie?"

"Yes," said Stevie, and ran over to the gate.

"Where have you been?"

"Up the hill to have a look at the fire." Stevie didn't notice that Peter looked miserable and was dressed in his best clothes.

"What's it like?" Peter asked.

Stevie pulled a long face. "Not much. Way over the mountains. Can't see anything 'cept a bit of smoke."

"There's no danger then?" said Peter.

"Danger?" squealed Stevie. That was a word for women. "It's only a bit of a fire," he said. "The fellas'll put it out."

"Putting out fires isn't easy on a day like this."

"You ever seen a fire?" said Stevie, with a faint touch of superiority.

"No."

"Well, I have. They put them out real easy. It's fun."

"That's not what Gran says," said Peter. "I've got to go home, back to town."

"We're going to the beach," said Stevie.

"Are you *still* going?"

Stevie looked surprised. "Course we are. Why not?"

"Well, the fire and everything. Isn't your dad afraid something'll happen?"

Stevie was disgusted. "Only scaredy-cats are afraid of fire."

"I'm not afraid," said Peter.

"Then what are you going home for?"

"Gran says I've got to."

"Go home 'cos of a *fire?* Gee whiz. Do they think you're a girl or somethin'?"

The enormity of the thought suddenly appalled Stevie, and it struck at Peter like a slap in the face. In a moment Stevie realized that he was peering over the top of the gate at an empty veranda. The slamming door left Peter's departure in no doubt. "How do you like that?" said Stevie. He thought it over, but couldn't make sense of it; so he skipped on homewards until he broke into a run.

"Do you know what?" he said, bursting in on his parents, "Peter's got to go home 'cos of the fire. That old Gran of his says he's got to go home."

"Now wait a minute, wait a minute . . . ." said his father. He was squatting on his haunches, mopping up water with a towel and wringing it out into a bucket. Stevie's mother was still in her dressing-gown, still strained-looking. Though Stevie didn't realize it, his mother and father had been having *words*.

"What's all this about?" Mr Buckingham said. "The fire's so far away that no one can see it . . . . Isn't it?" he asked, looking sharply at Stevie.

"Miles," said Stevie. "Miles and miles. Way on the other side of the mountains. Fancy makin' him go home!"

"Obviously," said Mrs Buckingham, "the Fairhalls know more about the fire than we do."

"How could they?" barked her husband. "We've got the phone on; they haven't. You've heard what the boy said. And you know what Bill Robertson said."

"I still want to know why the sirens went. If there's no danger, why sound the warning?"

"For heaven's sake, woman, I've told you. If there's a fire you put every available man onto it to get it out. If there's a brigade doing nothing in an area where there's no danger, you pull that brigade in, too. It's common sense. Our boys have gone to give them a hand, because they're not needed here."

"That's what you say, but I haven't heard it from anyone else. It comes too easy for my liking. With this wind blowing, it would be reckless to consider going away until we know that the fire is well and truly out. Now, the Fairhalls—"

"Since when have we set a course by the Fairhalls? You know what they're like with that boy. They'll ruin him . . . . Look, if it'll make you feel any better, we'll both get in the car and drive up to the top of the hill and see for ourselves. That's what we should have done in the first place."

Her shoulders drooped. She didn't like arguing in front of Stevie, and she didn't want him to see that she was frightened.

It was Pippa who turned their thoughts in another direction. Her face, flushed and panting, appeared suddenly pressed against the screen door to the kitchen. "Dad," she cried. "I can't find Julie."

"Oh, for heaven's sake!" Mr Buckingham threw the towel to the floor and straightened up with a hand pressed to the small of his back. "Has anyone ever been able to find Julie when she's in trouble? What's *that* to get excited about?"

Pippa opened the door and immediately knew she had walked in on an argument. How could people argue at a time like this? She was so breathless and so upset that the sob that welled up inside her couldn't be stopped. "Don't you understand?" she cried. "I can't find her. I can't find her, and there's a fire. She's lost, and there's a fire."

Mr Buckingham ran his fingers like claws through his hair. His patience had run its course. "Am I to be plagued all day by a bunch of hysterical females?" he shouted. "What's wrong with everybody? Now listen; the fire's not burning at the boundary fence; it's not burning at the end of the road; it's burning, if it's not already out, so many miles away that as far as we're concerned there may as well not be a fire. Now will everybody get a grip on themselves? Will you pull yourselves together? I dread to think what this house would be like in a real emergency. Julie's probably gone up to Grandpa Tanner's for a bit of sympathy. Did you think of that, Pippa? No, of course you didn't. So get yourself up there and bring her home. And you—" he turned on Stevie "—I thought you said that Pippa had found her? What do you mean by telling a lie like that?"

"Eh?" Stevie was astonished. He had believed with smug satisfaction that his father had been counting him as a man.

"I didn't say that. Did I, Mum? I didn't."

Mrs Buckingham was very pale and very much on her dignity. "I don't know what you said, and I'm sure your father doesn't know either. Pippa, Peter's going home. On your way back from Grandpa Tanner's will you call in and tell the Fairhalls that if Peter's ready by ten-thirty he can drive with us to the station. Come hail, come storm, come conflagration, your father is determined to go, so go we shall. I only hope, for his sake, that the house is still here when we get back."

4. State of Emergency

Lorna George failed to realize for a while that something was happening to her father. She was aware of his presence without consciously looking at him. She naturally thought that he was picking, doggedly and stubbornly, even though he must have known the fruit was useless; it was a ritual of defiance that meant nothing except that in some curious way it expressed his will to survive.

It was so hot that when she bent down her head swam. Perspiration ran into her eyes and beaded the backs of her hands. She could taste perspiration like tears; she could feel it tugging at her clothes. And oh, how she wished that John were around. Having John around was like having a strong arm about her shoulders. But John was on the road somewhere or other, what road she didn't know, driving the fire truck or perhaps even in the bush running out hoses. He mightn't be back for hours. If it was a bad fire he mightn't be back until the evening or the middle of the night. Once he had gone off to fight a fire somewhere and hadn't come home for two days. The thought was like a sigh. She even heard the sigh. It was a curious sensation, as if some unseen person, close by, had been listening to her thoughts. Then she realized that it was her father. He was a couple of rows away from her, three or four yards, staring at her. His eyes were glazed. She had never seen anybody look like that before. His mouth was open and he seemed unable to breathe. Then she saw him fall, just like a puppet without strings.

Lorna didn't cry out. She couldn't reach for him. Raspberries blocked the way. All she felt was a vast numbness, an inability to make a sound or a movement. She felt so small and the world about her seemed so large. The roaring, tossing trees seemed to reach to the sky. The world seemed to be a gigantic noise.

She was sure her father was dead. He seemed suddenly to have taken a long, long journey, leaving her alone and helpless in a violent world.

Pippa hurried up the hill to Grandpa Tanner's. She knew it was a waste of time. Grandpa wouldn't even be up. He was hardly ever up before eight o'clock or nine o'clock. Not that he slept. He merely lay there in his untidy old bedroom, with his eyes shut so that it would be easier to see things the way they had been when his farm was so beautiful that passers-by often stopped their cars to look at it, when strong and handsome children played in the garden, when Marjorie his wife kept a home so crisp and sparkling that people were heard to say, "You could eat your dinner off the floors." Anyway, Pippa couldn't imagine him lying there with his eyes open, for there was nothing to see but faded wallpaper and heavy old furniture in need of a polish and a bare electric-light globe hanging from the ceiling.

Pippa thought how terrible it would be to be old and lonely and to have nothing to get up for, not even a nice breakfast. Pippa knew that Grandpa wasn't very interested in food. She was sorry that he wasn't her real Grandpa because she wanted to love him that little bit more; and this was difficult when he wasn't her real Grandpa, for it was a right that belonged to other people: to his real grandchildren who sometimes came to see him.

Pippa was jealous of these real grandchildren, in a way. They were older children (many of them were grown up) and she didn't know them very well and didn't like them over much. One day one of them had said to her, "You're only nice to him because he might leave you some money." This had so upset Pippa that she hadn't visited Grandpa for weeks afterwards. She felt awful about it because she had always thought Grandpa was poor. She was only ten years of age when she said to him, "Please, Grandpa, don't leave me any money. It'd spoil everything." Now she was thirteen and still she wasn't sure that Grandpa hadn't left her anything, or whether Grandpa had enough money to leave anything to anybody; but she was surer than ever that if he did leave her something she'd give it away. Every time she thought of what that sharp-faced girl had said to her, even years afterwards, a cold and dark feeling grew inside her. It was the only unhappy memory Pippa had.

She knocked on Grandpa's back door. It sounded a firm and confident knock, but it wasn't. Pippa *knew* that Julie wasn't there. She *knew* that Julie was lost or hiding somewhere in the bush. Her father's attitude had made her angry. She felt she wanted to hit him. Her father could be a very nice man, but Pippa believed she was beginning to see him as a person, as a stranger might see him, not just as a once rather wonderful Dad. Sometimes, particularly in the mornings, he was a very disappointing person.

She knocked again, convinced that Grandpa had not heard her and probably wouldn't hear her anyway because he had the wireless going. She knew she was wasting precious time, that she should have been in the bush searching, should have bullied her family into helping her, should have gone to get Peter, perhaps Lorna as well, to help to search systematically. All she had got from her father was a snarl, a roughly spoken order. Julie, for all they knew, might even have been down a mine hole or caught up in blackberries somewhere, crying, scared to try to free herself because the thorns were as sharp as knives. There were bush cats, too—domestic cats run wild— that would attack even a man. Dad had a scar from his elbow to his wrist to prove it. And snakes, venomous black snakes and poisonous copperheads. Then Grandpa opened the door.

"Hullo, Pippa," he said.

He was dressed!

"Looking for Julie, I suppose?" he said.

"Yes," said Pippa blankly.

"Come on in then. We're having our breakfast."

"Breakfast," repeated Pippa, relieved; but somehow angrier than ever. It was unfair that her father had been right. It was all wrong that anyone who had cared so little should have been right.

"Would you like an egg?" said Grandpa. "We're having boiled eggs in egg-cups with flowers on them and toast and marmalade and milk with chocolate flavouring. Come on in. Don't stand there. We'll have a real party breakfast, the three of us, a going-away party."

"No," said Pippa. *"No!"*

Grandpa stared at her. "What is it, child? What's wrong?"

"Julie's a bad girl. She's a wicked, bad girl. I've been half out of my mind. I thought she was lost in the bush, and she's here! What's she doing here?"

"Goodness me, Pippa," said Grandpa.

"Julie's not going to have breakfast with you either. She's got to come home. You should have sent her home. She's been very naughty." Pippa had got to the stage of not knowing what she was saying. "I've been screaming all over the place for her. I've got into a row about her. It's not fair and she's been here all the time."

Suddenly Pippa ran away, crying, not because she was angry any more, but because she knew she was being rude and didn't know how to stop.

Peter and his grandparents sat down to breakfast. It was an enormous meal. It always was. Throughout their long lives the Fairhalls had lived well. Even in the bad years way back in the early thirties they had lived well, though everyone had thought they were hard up. The Fairhalls, years ago, had inherited from a distant relative an interest in a chain of shops. No one but the Income Tax Department knew of this inheritance.

Gramps was an enormous and florid man, completely bald, slow and ponderous. He hadn't always been that way; as soon as he had stopped working hard he had gone to fat. Beside him Peter looked so insignificant as scarcely to be real. A visitor arriving for the first time from another world might pardonably have mistaken them for members of two different species.

Gran was a big woman with shiny pink cheeks and a passion for getting up at five-thirty. This was something of a rite. Immediately the clock struck she was out of bed. Wild horses, she said, would not get her up a minute sooner, nor would they delay her a minute longer; and just before six, every day, in all seasons, the Fairhalls sat down to breakfast, ready for the sound of the six o'clock time signal on the radio, and the voice of the announcer reading the first news broadcast of the day.

In almost all things the Fairhalls were predictable, and any reasonably perceptive student of human nature could have foreseen their reactions to the vaguest threat of fire.

"We have experience of these things, boy," Gramps said. His voice, too, was enormous; even when he spoke quietly it had depth and breadth, like the ocean. "We have lived here for more than forty years. We know about fires, and if you have the least consideration for our feelings you will agree with the wisdom of our decision. It is our duty to send you home without delay. I am pained, boy, that you are allowing the thoughtless remarks of a stupid little thing like Stevie Buckingham to unsettle you."

Gramps was so positive, so overpowering.

"It's got nothing to do with Stevie," said Peter miserably. He couldn't look at Gramps. If he looked at him he knew he wouldn't be able to say anything. And it *was* to do with Stevie. really. It certainly had nothing to do with anything else: at heart he didn't care whether he went home or stayed, for Pippa would be gone, and without Pippa Ash Road would be dull and deadly. "But Stevie did say he couldn't even see the fire. He did say it wasn't stopping them from going on their holidays."

"If Buckingham goes," said Gramps, "he's an even bigger fool than I take him for."

"I'm thirteen," said Peter. "I'm not a baby any more. I want to stay."

"As far as I am concerned," said Gramps, "young persons of thirteen are more like babies than babies are. You're going home, boy. That's flat. Now be quiet or we'll miss the news. I will not have talk while I'm listening to the news."

"Yes," said Gran, "do be quiet. If there's a serious fire in these hills we want to hear about it."

". . . with the fire danger throughout the State near to an all-time high, disaster has struck overnight close to the city.

"Fierce fires are raging this morning in sight of the outer suburbs. Some are out of control in deep gullies and on steep slopes where they cannot be fought directly without risk of life. Three teenage boys are missing, and numerous homes have been destroyed. The pall of smoke from the fires is visible from many parts of the metropolitan area. It has been observed from ships at sea.

"The fires began in tinder-dry scrub country behind the town of Tinley shortly after one o'clock this morning. Whipped up by strong north-westerlies, flames spread rapidly, defeating the efforts of several rural and metropolitan brigades to contain them. Over three hundred fire-fighters are at present engaged in what the Country Fire Authority describes as 'a desperate attempt to save the foothills'.

"During a night of sudden terror in the Tinley district twenty-two homes were destroyed, and about thirty others are still in danger. No casualties have been reported, but concern is felt for the safety of three boys last seen in the Tinley area at about four o'clock yesterday afternoon. Mr K. Whitney, a Tinley shopkeeper, told police that three boys aged about fifteen bought supplies at his store yesterday afternoon and discussed the possibility of camping in the area known locally as McCullock's Gully. This area was ringed by fires soon after the main outbreak. A police search party entered the still-smouldering area at daybreak. The township of Tinley is considered to be safe at present, but a change of wind could suddenly and dramatically endanger it.

"This morning hundreds of acres of forest and grassland

between Tinley and Barkley are blackened, stock losses are
feared to be heavy, and hundreds of homes on the western
slopes of the ranges are expected to be threatened during the
next few hours. Police have ordered the evacuation of about
sixty families in the immediate path of the flames, and have
warned others to be ready to leave at a moment's notice. Inhabitants of townships farther up in the ranges are feverishly
widening firebreaks around their homes and damping down.
It is feared that strong winds and accompanying fierce up-
draughts above the inferno may carry burning twigs and ash
and exploding gases far beyond the limits of immediate danger
and produce fresh outbreaks. Townships miles from the front
line of the fire are preparing to fight for their existence. Sirens
have been wailing for half the night. Holiday-makers are
leaving the area, caravan parks have emptied, and the sick, the
elderly, and hundreds of children are already leaving the townships under police supervision. Public halls and churches clear
of the danger zone are being used for emergency accommodation.
Women's auxiliaries are caring for the evacuees, and army
field kitchens have been set up to provide meals for the fire-
fighters.

"The Country Fire Authority describes the outlook as
extremely grave. The weather forecast is for continuing strong
north to north-west winds and above-century heat with no relief
in sight. Heat-wave conditions may well continue for several
days.

"At five-thirty this morning the Country Fire Authority called
for two thousand able-bodied volunteers. Volunteers living in
hills districts are advised to report to their nearest fire station.
Volunteers approaching from the city are advised to travel by
train to the Barkley or Miltondale Railway Stations where fire-
fighting equipment will be issued. Groups will be transported
to threatened areas where they will be placed under the command of experienced officers. Volunteers are requested not to
drive private motor vehicles into bushfire areas. This could
lead to the needless destruction of vehicles or to the congestion
of roads required for the swift evacuation of residents. Roadblocks have been set up on all main roads into the threatened
areas. Only bona-fide residents and authorized personnel will

be permitted to pass these points. Volunteers are requested to dress in stout clothing, strong boots, and some kind of head-covering. The danger from snakes is high. Snakes fleeing from the flames have already been reported in significant numbers and several fire-fighters have received emergency treatment for bites.

"A spokesman for the Country Fire Authority said this morning that there is every indication that the fires are man-made. 'It is a tragedy,' he said, 'that has struck with bewildering speed and no useful purpose can be served by minimizing the risks involved. Crass stupidity or criminal negligence has led to a situation that only the utmost of human courage and ingenuity will bring under control. Every effort will be made to trace the person or persons responsible. They will be prosecuted to the limit of the law.' "

Peter knew it was useless trying to argue any longer.

Pippa, in a muddle of misery, sat at the roadside under the trees near Grandpa Tanner's gate. She half-thought that Julie would be sent after her; but Julie didn't come. She thought that perhaps Grandpa would have followed her, but he hadn't. She expected her mother or her father to be waiting in the middle of the road for news of Julie, but they weren't. She badly needed someone to make the move that would get life back onto an even keel. She couldn't go home and she couldn't go back to Grandpa. It was awful.

She looked up. Three boys were coming over the brow of the hill. They looked like fourth or fifth-formers—big fellows, two of them—and she had never seen any of them before. They were carrying heavy packs, and they were dragging their feet.

Pippa shrank from them; not because she was frightened of strangers, but because she knew her eyes were red. The scrub along the fence line was thick, and she slipped back into it. She knew the boys hadn't seen her, and she was sure they would pass by and never guess she was there. She knew it wasn't very lady-like, but anything was better than meeting strange boys, close up, the way she felt.

It wasn't long before she could hear their feet dragging in the gravel. They were not walking like boys at all, and they were not speaking to one another. It was odd: those dragging feet and no voices. As they went past she caught a glimpse of them. Three tired boys, haggard and very dirty. Two were limping. One had a soiled handkerchief tied round his arm like a bandage. The dirt on their clothes was mostly black—black streaks, black smudges, even scorch marks.

Pippa felt a quickening of interest and sympathy. She barely stopped herself from calling out to them. As soon as they were past, she found herself drawn irresistibly out of hiding, and she stood quite openly at the edge of the road, following them with her eyes.

They had come out of the fire; that was plain; but the fire was miles and miles away. What were they doing here in Ash Road? They trudged on past the Fairhalls' gate, then past her own gate, on down the hill, and never once looked back or apparently to either side.

She went after them, her own unhappy state of mind completely forgotten.

What an extraordinary thing it was. She should have spoken to them. She should have called after them. They may have been sick or something. It was queer.

"Pippa."

The sound of her name startled her.

It was Peter: Peter with a strained and hangdog look about him. But there was always something else about Peter, something extra, no matter how he looked: an intensity of feeling, an earnest desire to see into her mind and to please her no matter what her mood might be. She could see it in him now. Peter was so transparent. She found him rather tiresome at times. There were days when she would have loved him to have got good and mad with her, but Peter never lost his temper.

As for Peter, every time he saw Pippa it was a delight; just like meeting an exciting person for the very first time.

"Did you know them?" Peter said.

"The boys? Never seen them before."

Peter was glad about that, and said, "Must be fire-fighters, I reckon."

"No fires to fight down here," said Pippa, and remembered she had a message to deliver to Peter. "Mum says you can come with us if you like, when we go. About half-past ten. We've got to go through Miltondale, so we'll pass the station."

Peter looked away, half-ashamed that Pippa knew he was being sent home, and even more miserable about it now that he had to go into details. "I don't think they'll let me stay that long. I think they're going to take me soon as Gramps gets the car going. The battery's flat or something. Reckons I've been playing in it and left the ignition on. I didn't either. I bet he left it on himself. Gran's going all the way with me because Gramps says it's too dangerous for her to stay here."

"She's going too?" exclaimed Pippa.

"I'll bet he's always leaving it on. Serves him right for making me go home."

"But what's your Gran going for?" said Pippa.

"Eh?" said Peter. "Well you've heard about it, haven't you? All the houses being burnt down and everything?"

"No," said Pippa, suddenly irritated again. "And neither have you. That's what people always say when there's a fire. You shouldn't say things like that, Peter. It's silly."

"But it's true. It was on the radio just now. I heard it. Fellas missing and everything. Thousands of chaps fighting it, they say. It's all along the other side of the mountains."

Pippa stared at him in total unbelief. "How could it be?" she said. "They'd never let it get that big."

"But it is. They've got roadblocks up. They're evacuating townships. It's burning like mad and they can't put it out."

"You're making it all up. You're awful."

"Cross my heart, Pippa. I wouldn't tell a lie. Golly, I wouldn't tell a lie to you. Gramps says it's sure to come here. There's nothing to stop it, he says. He says if your Dad's got any sense he'll send you away, too, and Stevie and Julie, and that if he doesn't do it the police will anyway, any minute now. They'll be knocking on the door, he says. They'll just come and take you away."

"You're a big fibber," shouted Pippa. "Even if it got to the dam it couldn't come any farther."

"It can go around it."

"You're terrible, Peter. You're real *sick*. I just know you're making it all up."

She poked a stupid, tearful, frantic face at him, and suddenly ran away, down the road. Peter's heart almost broke; he felt the wrench inside him. "Pippa," he cried after her. Oh, gosh, he wouldn't see her again, probably for weeks or months. He couldn't take that picture of her away with him; not a contorted, frightened face like that. "Pippa," he shouted and started running after her, quite forgetting that he had promised not to set foot outside.

He caught her way past her own front gate; she had run straight past it. Peter was dismayed to find that she was really and truly sobbing. He didn't understand. She suddenly seemed like a stranger.

"Pippa," he said breathlessly, "please don't cry. Don't cry, Pippa. I'm sorry. I didn't mean to frighten you."

"You're horrid, Peter Fairhall. You *were* making it up, weren't you?"

"I don't know," he said, because he didn't know what to say. "In a way, I suppose . . . . I don't know. Honest, I don't know, Pippa . . . . No, of course I wasn't making it up."

She gritted her teeth and roughly broke his grip on her arm. "Leave me alone. Go away. I hate you."

"Golly, Pippa."

She ran away from him again, down the hill, and he sprinted after her. "Pippa," he cried. "Come back. Don't be silly."

5.   They Who Run Away

LORNA sat on the ground between the raspberry rows, nursing her father's head in her lap, stroking his brow, fighting to keep the panic off her face so that she might reassure him.

He was looking at her, speechlessly. It was frightening, but there was something very precious about it, like a sacred bond between them. He hadn't spoken a word for minutes. His only communication with her was through his eyes. It was hard to read them because they were dull, but she knew they were asking her not to leave him. She wanted to run for help, to ring for the doctor or an ambulance, but his eyes asked her to stay. She wanted to get out of his sight and out of his hearing so that she could let herself go. The sacred moment was turning into an agony.

"What is it, Dad?" she said. "Where does it hurt?"

He couldn't tell her.

"Dad," she said, "I must try to get John."

But his eyes wouldn't let her go.

"Please, Dad. Let me go for the doctor."

"In a little while," his eyes seemed to say.

So she nursed his head and tried to shade him from the sun. When she went for the doctor she would have to leave him in the sun because she was afraid that if she tried to move him she might kill him. She mightn't be able to move him, anyway, even though she wasn't a frail girl; she chopped the wood sometimes, when there wasn't a man around. She thought of herself chopping wood, and, strangely, that made her feel wretched. How lonely it would be, splitting sticks for the stove with only John and herself to cook for. She thought of all the nice things her father had done, forgot his irritability, thought of his lifelong battle to make ends meet. She thought, too, of her black despair when she had believed him to be dead.

"Dad, I must go. I couldn't bear to lose you. I'd never forgive myself if I could have saved you by trying. Please let me try to get some help."

It was one of the rare times in her life when she had reached him wholly and completely with her heart. She knew he was ready to let her go, so she fled up the rows towards the house, crying a little, confused because she wasn't exactly sure what to do.

When she got to the telephone she couldn't remember the doctor's number, and when she tried to turn over the pages of the directory her hands seemed as big and as clumsy as the stumps of trees. She could scarcely see the pages, didn't even know what page she was looking at. She screwed her eyes up and squinted, but she couldn't read the print. She had been in the brilliant sunlight for so long that she could not see in the gloom of the house. She stumbled to the nearest window and pulled on the blind. It crashed upwards violently and the tassel slapped round and round. She dropped the directory into the sudden pool of sunlight on the floor. She found the number and with a painful effort of will dialled it slowly and precisely.

It rang and rang and there was no answer. She hung up because she knew there wasn't going to be an answer. She fumbled with the directory again, turning to Miltondale, for that was where the ambulance had to come from. Again she dialled deliberately, though she was shaking from head to foot.

"Civil Ambulance Station," said a woman's voice.

"Oh," cried Lorna. She could hardly get her thoughts straight. "Oh, thank goodness. I want an ambulance please. I'm all on my own. It's my father."

"I'm sorry." The voice was firm, but not unkind. "You'll have to wait."

"Wait?"

"I'm sorry. We're handling an emergency here. Where are you ringing from?"

"From Prescott. I can't even raise the doctor."

"I'm very sorry, my dear, but it's the fires. You'll have to try to make other arrangements. We've really got troubles enough of our own."

"But my father—" Lorna felt overwhelmed.

"Every doctor in the hills is there, my dear, and every ambulance. There have been an awful lot of injuries, snake bites and burns and broken legs and heart attacks. All sorts of things. The fire's got to come first this morning."

"But my father—"

"Can you drive a car?"

"I'm only *fourteen.*"

"But can you drive?"

"No, of course I can't."

"What's wrong with your father?"

"I don't know. I don't know anything about these things. I think he's dying."

"Listen to me, dear. If you want to help your father you must be very brave and very calm and very sensible. I'll try hard to get a car for you, but it's not going to be easy. Everyone's gone to the fires. Just about everyone, because we're threatened here. We're evacuating the town. The fire's only a mile away. There's no guarantee that a car could even get through to you or that you could get through to the hospital. You really mustn't rely on me. It will be much better, much surer, if you call one of your neighbours. They're so much closer."

"But I live on a farm," cried Lorna. "I'm way near the end of a road. I'm three miles from the township. It's a quarter of a mile to the nearest neighbours, and even they're on holidays. I'm all alone. There isn't anybody, anywhere."

"There must be someone, my dear. Even if they're half a mile away they're much closer to you than we are. Now you really must control yourself. Give me your name and address quickly and I'll do my best, but you must *not* rely upon me. Please, please don't—"

Suddenly that was all. The line died. "Hullo," shouted Lorna. "Hullo, hullo. Don't go away . . . . Hullo . . . ."

The line was dead. Desperately, she dialled the number again. There was no ring. Something had happened to the line between Prescott and Miltondale and the ambulance didn't even have her address.

She dialled the Fire Station. The line was still open there, but no one answered, not even the base radio officer. She dialled the taxi service, but no one answered. She dialled the Buckinghams, but no one answered.

She put the phone down, and for a few moments covered her face with her hands. There was a fear in her, a foreboding, such as she had never known before. Now it was more than fear for her father lying down there in the raspberries, in the cruel sun. Now it reached out to the fire *threatening Miltondale*. What were they talking about? What sort of fire was that? And then the fear came right back to herself, to her aloneness.

She ran outside and looked into the sky in the west and the north. There was no smoke, nothing that really looked like smoke, only the smell of smoke and of dust, and the blistering heat.

Perhaps she could get help at the Fairhalls or from Grandpa Tanner. But Grandpa was so old and the Fairhalls were so slow and they didn't have telephones, anyway. She looked at her father's old car in the shed. How she wished she could drive it. But it was a one-man car; her father had always made that perfectly plain. It was "very hard" to drive, he said. Even John was forbidden to use it. Only one person could drive it properly and that was her father, her stubborn father who should have replaced it with a better one years ago. And even the tyres of her bicycle were flat. There was always something wrong with her bike. Everything was worn out. Nothing worked.

She ran down the paddock again, back to her father. He lay in the full sun, streaked with dust and sweat. She felt so sad for him, for a man so proud to be lying there like that. Even if it hurt him she would have to move him. She wiped his face on her dress, hooked her hands under his armpits, and dragged him into the narrow strip of shade at the foot of the raspberries. "Won't be long now, Dad," she said. "They're coming."

She ran back up the hill. She was beginning to feel sick as well as confused; her stomach was churning and the pulse was thumping tightly in her temples. She honestly doubted that she had the strength to run as far as the Fairhall's or to Grandpa Tanner. Her legs wanted to give way at the knees.

Suddenly she thought of Bill Robertson, and she lurched to a stop, panting, against the house. He was young and strong and had a big truck and was only a mile and a bit up the road and was on the telephone and was to deliver a drum of oil to her father that morning, anyway. She hadn't spoken to Bill Robertson more than three or four times in her life, but at once he seemed very close to her.

She hurried inside, looked up his number, and dialled it. Almost to her disbelief there was no answer. Where was everybody? What was the use of a telephone in an emergency if no one ever answered it? For an awful moment she felt that perhaps her father was meant to die. There were people who said that when one's number was up, it was up, and nothing could be done about it; that trying to prevent the passage of destiny was like commanding a river to flow backwards.

There was a knock on the door. It frightened her terribly, because there wasn't anyone, she thought, within miles. All sorts of sinister images flashed through her mind, things she had never thought of before. The knock seemed at this moment like a signal confirming that time was up for her father, or even like a signal from her father himself, as if his spirit as it passed by had paused for one last moment of contact with her.

The knock came again. It was, after all, an earthy, ordinary knock. How could it have been anything else? She felt ashamed, then widly elated. Now it seemed like an answer to a prayer.

She went to the door, and there, beyond the wire screen, silhouetted against the brilliant light, were the heads and shoulders of two real live men. One of them said, "Do the Pinkards live here?"

Then she saw they weren't men, but boys, strange boys, and that there were three of them. She pushed the door open, but was tongue-tied. When at last she spoke, her words flooded out in disorder, and the third boy, the one standing back, said almost in an undertone, "It's the wrong place. I told you it was. Let's scram."

"Don't go," she said sharply, suddenly afraid again.

The nearer two glanced at each other uneasily, and the third continued to back away. "Come on," he said insistently. "It's not Pinkards'. I said it was at the bottom of the hill."

"Do stay," appealed Lorna. She couldn't believe that anyone would leave her now. "I can't get a doctor and my father's ill. I can't get anybody. Nobody answers the phone."

The boy at the back said, "Do we look like doctors? Come on, fellas. Let's get out of here."

"You wouldn't *leave* me," cried Lorna. "You couldn't do that. He's down in the paddock, out in the sun. Can't you even carry him up to the house for me?"

"Look," said the boy at the back, not to Lorna but to the others, "we—can't—get—involved."

Lorna gaped at him. He didn't look that sort of boy. He looked tired and dirty, terribly dirty; they all did; but he had a nice face. The face didn't go with the words that came out of it. Nothing fitted. Not even the roughness that was in his voice. Nor did it make sense that the others seemed inclined to do as he said. They were so much bigger and burlier than he was. The biggest was like a man, except for his face. It didn't seem right that the most boyish of them should be their spokesman, should decide their actions. Lorna was desperate. She had to hold them.

"There's an old door in the shed," she said, almost fiercely. "It'll do for a stretcher. We can each take a corner." She glared at the boy in the rear. "You're a fine sort of gentleman, you are!"

"Come on, Graham," said the big one. "We've got to do it. Haven't we?"

Pippa walked and stumbled down the road with her eyes fixed ahead She longed to sit down somewhere and have a good weep, or go home, but she couldn't turn back, couldn't even stop, while Peter was there. She hated him and he wouldn't stop following her. He was like a dog. If he had started yelping and snapping round her ankles she wouldn't have been surprised. "Go away," she said. "You make me sick."

Peter didn't answer back; he stuck stubbornly behind her, though he had a suspicion that he was "cheapening" himself (whatever that may have meant), that if he really valued his "dignity" he would do as she wished. But there were things more important to Peter than the bewildering adult standards of conduct his parents and grandparents talked about and tried to impose upon him. Nothing was more important to Peter than Pippa's goodwill. He had never had a real fight with her before. It was a disastrous thing, as if he had been caught in a sinking ship and was powerless to save himself. It seemed that the only way to get back into a happy frame of mind was to be close to her when her humour changed; for surely her anger had to run out. This half-haughty, half-frightened girl in front of him was not like Pippa at all.

"You're still there, are you?" she said. "You're like a little puppy dog. Do they call you Fido at home?"

Pippa had not forgotten what the argument was about; she had seized upon it as something to be pursued to the bitter end, as a way of being rid of Peter Fairhall for good and all. Then she saw at the side of the road the three haversacks the heavy-footed boys had carried down the hill. She was instantly, if vaguely, curious and was surprised to see that she had come abreast of the Georges' gateway, that she was opposite the path flanked by cyprus trees that ran for about a hundred yards to the Georges' house.

"Good-bye," she said suddenly. "Good riddance. I'm going to see Lorna." She scarcely changed her stride, merely pivoted on the sole of her shoe.

"*No*," pleaded Peter.

For at once she was out of reach. The road was as much his as anybody's and he could pursue her there, but he couldn't take the argument through the Georges' gateway. Other people would straightaway be involved; it wouldn't be private any more. She'd got away from him!

He had been so sure that it would all work out. It hadn't.
It had ended with nasty words and with a pain so deep that
the world around him blurred and the details of earth and
scrub and trees for a few moments merged into a uniform
colour, a nameless colour that looked like misery. Then it
separated again into its components, and not far from his feet
were the three haversacks dumped in the tall, dry, wiry grass
at the edge of the roadside ditch. These became of absorbing
interest to him, though for a while he didn't really observe them.
He could see that they had come out of the fire, that the fire
had been so close to them that it had left its mark upon them,
that the packs were partly burnt, and that two of the sleeping-
bags strapped to them were not fit to be used again. They
triggered a strange response in him. He felt he knew about
these haversacks, that they were not new to him, that they had
reappeared out of some past or half-forgotten experience. Three
campers. Three teenage boys missing in the fire . . . .

He had never doubted for a moment that his deduction was
the right one. He *knew*.

There was in him, too, another bridge of understanding,
another flash of perception. Pippa had followed them down the
road. Pippa had followed them through the Georges' gateway.
In some obscure way they had created the division between
Pippa and himself; and he began to feel against them the stirrings of a positive dislike.

They *were* the missing boys. And they were missing not
because they had been burnt to death in the fire but because
they had got away from it. And for what reason would they get
away from it? Certainly not for the reason that applied to himself. They were on their own; they were free agents; and for
that, too, Peter resented them and envied them and wanted to
strike at them. Surely if they had had nothing to hide they
would have stayed to fight the fire? And what did they have to
hide but the fact that they had started it?

Rarely had Peter seen anything so clearly. Never had the
processes of his mind brought him so swiftly and surely to a
conclusion. That he had based it on the flimsiest of evidence
never occurred to him. He *knew*.

He didn't rush through the Georges' gateway; that was not

his nature; he started off down the path nevertheless, frightened
of those three big boys, but not so frightened that he was afraid
to face them in front of Pippa.

They put the door down in the shade at the back of the house,
and Lorna dropped on one knee beside her father. She didn't
know what to do next. She ran her fingers nervously across his
brow and said, "I'll get a pillow."

As soon as she had disappeared into the house Graham
hissed at the others: "You're crazy. You're plumb crazy. Now
look what you've done. How are we supposed to get out of this
lot? We're hooked."

Harry and Wallace glanced at each other and at the sick
man at their feet. Harry was tight-lipped. "It's just one of those
things," he said.

"Yeh," agreed Wallace. "No one's laughin', Graham. It's
like Harry says."

Lorna clattered out with the pillow in her hand.

"Here, give .it to me," said Harry, anxious to get her out of
the way again for a moment. "You'd better get a blanket, too."

"It's too hot for that," said Lorna.

"We don't know for sure, do we? We don't know what's
wrong with him. At least we're on the safe side if we cover him."

"All right," said Lorna and went inside again. Whether it
was the right or the wrong thing to do, it was at least something
to do.

Harry fluffed the pillow up and pushed it under the old
man's head. Graham mumbled, "We were safe. I just know
we were safe."

"We still will be," growled Wallace, "if you'll shut up."

"We'd got all this way," sighed Graham.

"Yeh, yeh."

Not one of them really knew how he was managing to stand
up or how he had managed to walk more than fourteen miles.
Fear and fright and dismay had pushed them past a sensible
limit. What a nightmare the hours of darkness had been,
hiding from passing traffic, dodging lights, sometimes running
with their packs jolting and jarring and chafing at them. Their
feet were like balls of fire. And their shoes had been in Harry's

pack all the time. Harry had bundled them up and stuffed them in his pack and hadn't even known he had done it.

Lorna brought the blanket and Harry took it from her. At that moment Pippa came round the side of the house.

She met Graham's eyes first. "He's nice," she thought. But Graham didn't notice Pippa for what she was or wasn't; he saw her as just one more hazard to be overcome, one more person who might take news of what he had done to the authorities or to his parents, one more reason why he had to get away by himself. He didn't want even Harry or Wallace. Much of what had happened was Harry's fault, anyway. "We're going to stick together," Harry had said, while they were still hiding not far from the fire. "We'll make for the Pinkards' straightaway. No one's there. All we've got to do is find the place. Jerry said if we got there before he did to make ourselves at home. That's good enough for me. It's the perfect place to lie low."

Harry had meant it for the best, but it had been a mistake, for it had turned them into a recognizable and fugitive group of three. They should have separated and agreed to meet up again at the Pinkards' in a couple of days. Graham was sure that guilt was stamped indelibly upon him. He was sure that the first keen eye, the first searching look would imply, "You did it, didn't you?" If the daughter of this sick man had not been so afraid for her father's life she surely would have spotted it herself. Now there was this new girl, this keen-eyed, alert girl. Graham felt instantly that she was as sharp as a tack, but apparently she wasn't, for her glance moved swiftly from him to Lorna and from Lorna to old man George. "Lorna," she cried, "what's happened to him?"

Lorna stared at her. "Where'd you come from? I've been ringing your number. Everybody's number. I couldn't get an answer anywhere."

"Mum's there," said Pippa, not fully understanding. "Dad's there. Stevie, too, I think."

"But no one answered. I rang and rang. Oh, Pippa, my dad's awfully sick. I don't know what I would have done if these boys hadn't turned up. I thought your dad could drive him to hospital, but I couldn't get an answer. They're not home, Pippa. Honest, they're not—"

"But they are—"

"I can't get the Robertsons, I can't get the Fire Station, I can't get the doctor or a taxi or an ambulance or anything. People just don't answer. Where is everybody?"

"They must be there," insisted Pippa. "They've got all the packing to do. We haven't even had breakfast yet. You must have dialled the wrong number."

"But I didn't.

"Well let me try."

"Try if you want to, but I'm telling you they're not there."

The boys, prompted by a single thought, found themselves looking at one another, for the girl called Pippa followed the girl Lorna indoors. "Right!" said Harry.

As one, they scuttled round the side of the house and took a short cut across a garden bed towards the path. Then they saw Peter, and Peter saw them. They almost ran him down.

They halted a couple of paces apart, Peter, startled, no longer even partly sure of himself, confronted by Wallace and Harry, each aghast, but apparently threatening in their attitude—boys that Peter knew instantly and instinctively to be his enemies— and by Graham. Graham was weak with fright and gasped aloud. If only they had walked! Now their guilt was declared so positively they might as well have shouted it from the roof- tops. Innocent people didn't leap like scalded cats across garden beds.

But it was Peter who ran. The boys were so big; they looked so strong. He bolted, afraid that they were going to set upon him. Peter feared violence more than anything; he would go to any lengths to avoid a fight. He didn't stop running until he reached the road, and when he looked back the three boys were not to be seen. The only person in sight was someone who looked like Stevie, a long way up the hill, waving to him.

But the bigger boys were still there; they had gone to earth like frightened rabbits. They couldn't see Peter any more than he could see them. The roaring trees along the road and the path and round about them concealed them from one another, but only visually. In the minds of the three boys every tossing leaf was a spying eye, an accusing eye, and the difficulty of covering up their guilt was beginning to look overwhelming. They were so dog-tired that the situation was beyond them. They couldn't think straight, not even clever Harry could think straight, and Wallace's mind was a frightened blank waiting for a lead. Running away from the fire had only proved their guilt; it hadn't made them safer at all. And it wasn't that Graham had meant to start the fire; it had been such an innocent accident. But who'd believe them now? All the alibis they had invented seemed so feeble and so futile. Everyone would know now that they hadn't spent the night at the Pinkards', and if they couldn't face up to a few unsuspecting children how were they to face suspicious parents or angry officials.

Graham felt evil and deceitful and full of remorse because he had failed to help that poor girl willingly. She had looked such a nice girl. And why would an undersized boy of about thirteen take such fright? Graham was relieved that the boy had taken fright, but it still didn't make sense. Were all Graham's feelings beginning to show? "What do you think?" he said, in a half-choked voice. "Will I give myself up? It'll be so much easier if I do."

"Of course you won't give yourself up!" Harry's were angry words and Graham wanted them to be. He wanted Harry to drive the thought away, to kill it. "We can't worry ourselves about a kid. He got a fright, that's all, same as us. We haven't done murder or anything. The way you act anyone would think we had."

But they had lost the opportunity of escape: the girls had come to the side of the house: in sight of them and in hearing range if voices were raised. Perhaps the boys could still walk away as Graham had wanted to do in the first place, but that would be more cold-blooded now than it would have been then. Wallace said with a touch of bravado, "Why should they guess anythin'? Why should they find out anythin' if we don't tell them?"

"But that kid," said Graham. "He acted like he knew something. He was scared stiff."

"He got a fright," repeated Harry, belligerently. "So did we. He's gone now, anyway. I bet he hasn't stopped running yet."

"Well, what about our packs?"

"What about them?"

"They're up on the road for everyone to look at."

"Yeh," said Wallace. "You blokes see to the girl. I'll get rid of the packs. I'll hide 'em somewhere."

"Let me," said Graham breathlessly.

Harry looked at him, perhaps too closely, but believing he understood Graham's earnest desire to continue avoiding people if he could. "Okay. You do it. But remember where you hide them."

Graham, trembling from head to foot, headed for the gateway with all the haste his sore feet could summon. Pippa made a move, afraid that the boys were all going to melt away before her eyes. "Lorna wants some more help," she called and took a couple of steps towards them. "Are you going to give it to her?"

Pippa took a couple more steps, hesitantly, not sure of herself or whether these two big fellows were nice boys all dirtied up or a couple of toughs. Another time she probably wouldn't have thought of it, but the day itself was so violent. The wind that buffeted her was nerve-racking in a way; and her passionate argument with Peter was still in her mind like an ugly fright from which she had not recovered, and the shock of looking into Mr George's face was something she would not quickly forget. What an awful morning it had been, from the very first moment; as if she were living a day in the life of another person, as if all the circumstances of this day simply didn't belong to her. Even the monotonous buzz of the telephone that her parents had not answered. And why should these boys hold back? Why should they be as Lorna had said they were? "They do act funny, Pippa," Lorna had said. "Even when they helped me carry my dad they wouldn't look me in the eye."

Pippa took two or three more steps, and suddenly felt that she had ventured as close as any sensible person would dare. "Have you been fighting the fire?" she said.

It was a question they didn't want to answer but had to answer. "Yeh," said Wallace, "that's right. Worn to a frazzle, too."

"You're tired?" said Pippa.

"Ready to drop," agreed Wallace, visibly slumping.

"Is that why you've been acting funny?"

Harry shrugged. "I wouldn't say we're acting funny."

"I told Lorna that you'd been fire-fighting, that that's what was wrong with you."

"Nothing's wrong with us."

"Where's he going?" Pippa glanced in the direction Graham had taken.

"Nowhere," said Harry. "He'll be back."

They didn't sound like toughs, not really. "Lorna wants help to carry her father up the road," said Pippa. "We've got to get him to my place. My dad doesn't answer the phone, but I know he's there."

"You mean carry him on that door?"

"I suppose so."

"How far is it?"

"About a third of a mile."

"Crumbs . . . . When Wally said we're ready to drop he meant it, you know." Harry knew he shouldn't have said more, but he couldn't stop himself. "We've been fighting fires all night. We wouldn't be here now except they sent us away for a rest."

"Did they send you as *far* as this?"

"Yeh," said Wallace. He couldn't resist the temptation to impress. "That's right. We're down this way to have a rest and keep an eye on things. Eh, Harry?"

"Sort of," said Harry, uneasily. "Wouldn't it be easier for you to get your dad to come down here?"

"It would be if he's home. But if he's not home we'll have to get someone else. The Fairhalls, probably."

"Who are the Fairhalls?"

"They live opposite my place. They've got a car, too."

"It's no farther then—is it?—to walk to the Fairhalls than it is to your place?" said Harry.

"I suppose not."

"Well, what's the use of killing ourselves struggling up that hill with the door and all? Doesn't make sense, does it? You don't need us at all, do you?"

Pippa couldn't quite follow the circle the conversation had

taken. She turned back to Lorna with a confused shake of her head and Lorna said heatedly, "I told you they wouldn't help. I told you they were running away from something. They're not worn out from fighting fires, they're worn out from running away."

Wallace was suddenly frightened and aggressive. "What's that you say?" he shouted.

"You heard what I said," Lorna yelled. "My brother's a fire-fighter and he's fighting them now. If he was here he'd punch you on the nose. You're not fire-fighters. You're just nothing. Get off my father's property before I set the dog on you."

"What dog" sneered Wallace. "I don't see any dog. Y'haven't got one."

"I have, too," screamed Lorna. "Blackie. Blackie! Here, Blackie!"

Wallace saw red. Somehow this screaming girl seemed to be the whole reason why their wonderful holiday had turned into a nightmare. He grabbed at a garden stake and dragged it out of the ground, uprooting the plant with it, and brandished it at her. "Put a dog on me," he yelled, "and I'll beat the daylights out of it. I'll beat 'em out of you, too."

"Put that stick down!" shouted Harry across Wallace's threats. "Are you crazy?"

Pippa stared in astonishment and fright, sure that she should have been running for her life but unable to move, blankly dismayed that she had become a part of something that wasn't supposed to happen to nice people. All she could produce was a plaintive cry against the wind: "Peter Fairhall! Peter!" Lorna, frightened and defiant, continued shouting taunts. "You're probably thieves or something. You're probably runaways from a Home or something. Blackie! Blackie! Where are you, Blackie?"

"This is stupid. This is mad," bellowed Harry. "All right. We'll carry him for you. We'll do whatever you want."

"You'll do nothing for me. I wouldn't have you touch my father. Get off this property or I'll ring the police. Blackie! *Blackie!*"

Wallace dropped the stake at his feet almost as if it had

turned red-hot in his hands. He seemed suddenly to hear his own father, "You're as strong as a man, Wallace. Hold that strength back or it'll land you in trouble. You must learn to control yourself or you'll bite off more than you can chew." And it had happened. He didn't know how or why, except that the urge to use his strength violently had been overpowering, had seemed the only way to break out of something he couldn't understand. There wasn't a dog; the dog didn't come; but the girl still called for him. She wouldn't have kept on calling if there hadn't been a dog, and Wallace knew from the way she called that it'd be a big dog. He was afraid it would leap upon them out of the trees like a sleek black panther, and he gasped, "Run for it. Quick. She's crazy."

In that moment Harry almost despised Wallace. But it was only for a moment between the numbing confusion of the abusive exchange and a sudden stinging pain behind his left knee. Harry fell, from the shock of the pain and the hurt of it. He thought he had been shot, but it wasn't a bullet; it was a stone as big as a golf ball that little Stevie Buckingham had snatched from the path on the run and hurled with all his strength at Wallace. Harry went down with such a sharp cry, and the crack of the stone was so pronounced, that Wallace, too, thought Harry had been shot, and the last fires of his dangerous mood went out. He was suddenly cold and physically afraid. Muscles and sinews were no match for bullets.

He spun on his heel and confronted not a man with a gun but a boy, a boy no more than chest-high, coming at him like a terrier. Wallace was so surprised he couldn't protect himself. A sharp-toed shoe cracked into his shin, and with an anguished yell he reeled backwards, pummelled by the boy's fists, frightened to lash out in case he hit too hard, his feelings a mixture of amazement and alarm and honest admiration for the courage of the little fellow. "Bully," the boy was screeching. "Bully, bully, bully." And with every screech he landed another kick or another scratch or another punch on Wallace's stinging body.

"Stevie," Pippa shouted. "Stop it! He's not fighting you, Stevie. You've won, Stevie. Stop it!"

6. Evacuation

GRAHAM was sure that at last he was safe. It had been a close thing, but he was certain now that all the excitement had had nothing to do with him. He had scarcely pulled the haversacks into the scrub near the fence line when he heard a voice on the wind. What the voice said he didn't wholly hear but rather pieced together.

"Peter Fairhall. I saw you. Come on out, Peter Fairhall. Your Gramps'll chew your leg off if you don't go home."

It had given Graham a bad moment, and it had taken him a while to realize that it was not his own name on the air: names didn't count for much when a fellow was on the run.

"What'cha hidin' for, Peter? Your Gramps wants you, Peter."

It was a busy little boy, pattering down the hill, sometimes pausing to call again. "Better go home, Peter Fairhall, or he'll wring your blitherin' neck. That's what he's sayin', Peter."

Graham couldn't understand how anyone could have seen him; he had taken such care not to expose himself to the open vista of the road. He had frozen; he had shrunk into the scrub.

"I know you're there, Peter Fairhall." The boy had taken a stone from the road and pitched it into the timber fifty yards or so farther up the hill. "You're a real scaredy-cat, aren't you, Peter Fairhall?" And he had come on again, calling, "Pippa!

Where are you, Pippa? Mum wants you, Pippa," and had
turned at last into the gateway, not a great distance from where
Graham was hidden, unaware of the eyes that followed him as
he skipped down the path, unaware even of the violence that he
was about to stumble upon.

Graham had grabbed his own pack then and darted along
the fence line from bush to bush until clear of the risk of being
seen from the house. Then he had run, he wasn't sure where,
except that it was away from the road, right away, he hoped,
from the direction of Pinkard's place, away from any place that
might draw people. He had to be on his own so that he might
give way, that he might lie down, that he might tear his shoes
off to ease the agony in his feet, that he might even go to sleep.
He didn't want to find Wallace and Harry again. He didn't
care if he never saw them again as long as he lived.

He came down into a gully where a creek was flowing. It
was no cooler than open ground, but it was private. He thought
he could hear an engine beating somewhere; it was a long way
off and the wind made its direction uncertain. But the trees
were tall and the bush was thick and there was water in the
creek and enough food in his pack to keep him alive for days.
The hiking-tent was in his pack, too, so at least he would be able
to get under cover at night. He felt vaguely that he was going
to live out his years beside this creek. He would never go back
into the world, never face his parents, never stand up in court
to hear himself accused and sentenced. Nor would he have to
worry himself sick about Maths B again.

He eased the pack to the ground and collapsed beside it,
panting. Part of him wanted to cry, but something told him
that he had to cling to what shreds remained of his self-respect;
He unlaced his shoes and gradually, painfully, withdrew his feet
from them. His feet were swollen and blistered and the skin
was broken in several places. They were awfully dirty. They
were awful to look at, and he stretched them out in front of him
and stared at them. He wanted to look somewhere else, but
couldn't. Oh, his feet. His poor feet. How had he walked on
them? And run on them?

He knew he should dress them, should wash them in the
creek, should do something to them, but he was too tired to do

anything but sit and unwind, and wonder. He knew he was going to sleep and there was nothing he could do to prevent it; he drifted off, half-sitting, half-lying against his pack.

Although Peter wasn't far away, he had lost sight of Graham. He knew Graham was in the gully somewhere, but exactly where he could not determine. It was the gully at the bottom of the Georges' place, very dense in parts, though farther along the fire brigade had burnt through it in the spring. He realized that he had missed his quarry somehow, had either gone past him or been eluded by him. It was an uncomfortable feeling, for there was always the possibility that now it was he who was being followed. He scuttled for open ground, for the edge of the huge carrot paddock where the sprinklers were turning, and stood there, disconsolate and undecided.

He didn't really know what he was up to, couldn't convince himself that he had followed Graham for any real purpose at all. He was trying to tell himself that it had been the brave and manly thing to do, but what was brave and manly about it? What was it supposed to achieve? How could it impress Pippa when she didn't know about it? Perhaps he had done it because of Stevie's taunt, or because of the stone that Stevie had tossed so close to where he had been hiding. He had only wanted to prove himself, but all he had done was deepen his misery. It was terrible being so weak and useless. It was awful being the kid who had to go home. And the wind was frightening him. It just never stopped. It was an unceasing blast. And smoke was up there now, clearly present in the sky. He hadn't noticed it before.

Stevie dropped back, drawing great breaths, still sobbing from the rage that had not entirely left him, feeling in its place the advance of a growing weakness. He looked a very little boy, almost too exhausted to stand, afraid that something dreadful was going to happen to him, that he was about to be beaten with a stick or a hard hand. From head to toe he drooped, and Pippa rushed to him and thrust an arm protectively round his shoulders. She felt for him as she had never felt before, a warm and admiring love, and she clutched him to her side and said to him, "Good boy, Stevie. Good boy, Stevie," and she glared at Wallace leaning sheepishly against the wall of the house and at Harry, still on the ground, flexing his injured leg and vigorously rubbing it. "Aren't you ashamed of yourselves?" she said to them.

"Yeh," said Wallace, who was in the humour to agree with anything and everything.

Harry raised himself to his feet, wincing. "Crumbs," he said. "That hurt."

Words, then, became useless; they stood in an embarrassed silence, not knowing how to break it. Blackie, the missing dog, came into the picture belatedly, with his tail between his legs. He must have heard Lorna from a great distance, for he was distressed and panting and muddy. Perhaps he had been in the creek or chasing rabbits in the carrots where the sprinklers were turning. Lorna, still on the defensive or the attack—she was not sure which—hooked her fingers through his collar.

It was Harry who finally broke the silence, awkwardly and selfconsciously. He knew it was time to speak, for the awful tension had gone, and he didn't want people to be thinking unkindly of him any longer. "I'm so sorry about this," he said hesitantly, "but we're not criminals or anything. Honest we're not. We've had an awful night. I just don't know what came over us . . . ."

He looked to Wallace for support, but he should have known better. Expressing the finer points was not Wallace's strength. All he could say was "Yeh."

"We're on holidays," Harry went on. "We go to Osborne High School in town. We're friends of Jerry Pinkard's. I'm Harry McAuley and he's Wallace Martin. I—I was captain of Form 3A this year . . . . Please don't be frightened of us. We're not thugs or anything."

"We're not frightened of you," said Lorna.

"Wallace is a good chap, you know, a real good sport. He's in all the teams and everything. He's a real star. I'll bet he's just as sorry as I am."

"Yeh," said Wallace.

"But we *are* in trouble, real trouble. We did an awfully silly thing. Don't ask us what, please." Harry couldn't find the words he wanted. Nothing sounded right. "We do want to help you, honest we do, but please don't tell anyone we're here. We'll probably get sent to prison or something. We didn't mean it to happen. It was all an accident . . . . It's spoilt our holiday and everything . . . ."

"I'm sorry," said Lorna. "But you couldn't have done anything that bad, surely?"

"It's terrible. It's awful . . . ." And suddenly it was out. "We—we—started the fire!"

"You *didn't*," cried Pippa.

"We didn't mean it to happen. It was an accident. It was so quick. We tried so hard to get it out . . . . We nearly got trapped . . . . We panicked . . . ."

"You lit the fire," cried Lorna. *"You* lit it!"

"He didn't neither," yelled Wallace. "He didn't do any such thing. It was my fault, and Graham's. It didn't have anythin' to do with Harry. Harry was asleep."

Harry hadn't meant to say it. He couldn't believe it had come out of his own mouth. And yet saying it somehow made him feel better. It was like a bad headache suddenly going away—until he looked at Stevie. Stevie was squinting at him with a twisted face. Harry had forgotten the little chap. Perhaps the two older ones would keep the secret, but how could he expect it of Stevie? Harry was suddenly confused again, wishing with all his heart that he could call back what had been said, that he could erase it from his own memory and from the memory of others. He felt cornered, lost. "Look," he said. "Your dad. We'll carry your dad for you. We'll take him wherever you say. Anywhere. And if anyone wants to know who we are, just tell them we're stopping with the Pinkards." He looked at Stevie. "You, too. Don't tell. Please don't tell anyone."

"Don't tell 'em what?" Stevie was still squinting at Harry. What had been said was just a flood of words to him. He didn't know what fire they were talking about. The only fire he knew of was on the other side of the mountains; and how could they possibly have lit that if they were with the Pinkards?

"The fire," Harry explained anxiously. "Don't tell them we lit it."

"What fire?" exclaimed Stevie.

Pippa squeezed him suddenly to her. "You must have hit him too hard with that stone, Stevie. He's all mixed up, isn't he?"

"I'll say," said Stevie. "He's real silly. I reckon he ought to go and sleep it off. He's stark, ravin' bonkers. And what's he talkin' about Dad for? Dad doesn't need carryin'. He'd have to run awful hard to catch him now."

"Not our dad," explained Pippa. "Lorna's dad."

"Oh," said Stevie. "Well, that's different. 'Cos Dad's gone. He couldn't very well carry *him*. What's Lorna's dad want carryin' for?"

"He's sick, Stevie . . . . But where's our dad gone?"

"With all the fellas. Mr Robertson came in his truck and picked Dad up and away they went. It was full of fellas?"

"But *where*, Stevie? Where have they gone?"

"To the big fire near Miltondale, of course. It was on the wireless and everything. You know."

"But I don't, Stevie. I don't know what you're talking about."

"Gee. You don't know much, do you?"

"It's right, Pippa," said Lorna. "That's why I couldn't get an ambulance. They said they were evacuating Miltondale."

"*Evacuating?*" cried Harry. "But Miltondale's miles from the fire. The fire's at Tinley."

"That's the one," said Stevie.

"Miltondale?" said Wallace incredulously. "It can't be the same fire."

"It is, you know," declared Stevie. "It's at Miltondale and Campbell Heights and Hughes and Mount Stewart. It's gone right along the mountain."

"It couldn't have," wailed Wallace.

"All the people are leavin' the townships." Stevie began to feel very important. "Hundreds of policemen directing the traffic and everything."

"Oh, Stevie," said Pippa, recalling with a sense of guilt and discomfort her row with Peter. "You couldn't have heard right."

"I did. Mum's gone, too. Old miseries they are. Wouldn't take *me*."

"Mum! What do you mean, Mum's gone?"

"All the ladies have gone. Mum took the car with Mrs Fairhall and Mrs Robertson and they were going to call for others on the way. They're all goin'.."

"What on earth for?"

"To look after the people of course."

"*What* people?"

"All the people that are comin' down from the mountains. They've got them in the public hall and the church halls and at the football ground. All the kids and all the ladies. They've gone in to make breakfast for them and everything."

"This is the silliest thing I've ever heard of. You don't know what you're saying."

"I do, you know," said Stevie haughtily. "I've been lookin' all over for you, to tell you. Mum sent me to tell you to come home because you haven't had any breakfast and to pack up the things you want to take in case we have to evacuate as well, and to stuff some rags in the downpipes and fill up all the spouts with water. Lots of things she wants you to do. You'd better come, too. She was awful cross 'cos you didn't come home with Julie. Grandpa Tanner had to bring her home and Grandpa said you were performin' like a primagonga. What were you performin' for, Pippa?"

"Where's Julie now?" Pippa asked.

"Gone back to Grandpa's again. Grandpa's lookin' after her. He's lookin' after Mrs Robertson's baby, too. What were you performin' for, Pippa?"

"None of your business," said Pippa sharply, and looked suddenly to Lorna. "What on earth are we going to do about your dad?"

There were times when Lorna was so sure of herself, so competent; but not now. "Everything seems to be against him, Pippa. It doesn't seem fair. We seem to be so cut off."

"Well, I'm not going to leave you. I don't care what Mum says."

"Mum says you've got to keep your ear open for the phone, too. Just in case she want to get in touch with you."

"Be quiet, Stevie."

" 'Cos if there's a wind-change or anythin' the fire might get good and mad and we might have to get out quick."

"Stevie, *do* be quiet."

"Cor," said Stevie, "a minute ago I was a bloomin' hero."

"Look," said Harry, "aren't you forgetting these Fairhall people? Or have they gone, too?"

"Well?" said Pippa to Stevie.

Stevie sighed. "I told you Mrs Fairhall had gone with Mum and Mr Fairhall's tryin' to start his bloomin' old car so he can take Peter home."

"What's wrong with his car?"

"It won't go!"

"And Peter's with him, I suppose?"

"I don't know. Not when I saw Mr Fairhall last. He was spittin' chips because Peter had gone away." Stevie's thoughts turned back a few minutes. "Though I reckon I saw Peter on the road when I was comin' down the hill. But he ducked into the bush and wouldn't answer."

"It might have been Graham," said Harry.

"Yeh," said Wallace. "What about Graham? Where is he? Shouldn't take him as long as this to shift a few packs."

"Look," said Harry, "if Stevie saw Graham duck into the bush, that explains it. Graham'll be hiding. You know the way he feels about everything. Unless it *was* this Peter. I guess he was that other kid—the one that took off like a jack-rabbit."

"I didn't see this Graham fella," said Stevie. "Not unless his legs are as skinny as Peter's."

"Graham's not skinny."

"It was Peter then."

"It doesn't matter about Graham or Peter," cried Lorna. "What are we going to do about my dad? He's probably dying, and all we do is talk, talk, talk. We've got to do *something!*"

And they looked at one another again. In the hearts of them all, except Lorna, there was perhaps the thought that if they didn't dwell on the problem it would go away.

"It's wicked," said Lorna, "not doing anything."

Harry shrugged helplessly. "Where do we start?"

Wallace said, "Does that old car I saw in the shed go? If it does I might be able to drive it."

"Can you *drive?*" asked Lorna.

"Yeh," said Wallace, surprised by her vehemence.

"Well why didn't you so say so?"

"You didn't ask, did you? And I thought the car wasn't any good or you would have mentioned it. It'd be the first thing anyone would think of."

"Easy does it," Harry said. "You can't drive."

"I can try, can't I? All we've got to do is get it movin' and keep it movin'. If my mother can drive I reckon I can. And I've watched Dad. I've sneaked a drive here and there. I'll get him to hospital all right. All I need is someone to show me the way."

"I'll do that," cried Stevie, and excitedly led the rush.

Grandpa Tanner walked from his back door to that spot down the slope a bit from which he could see through the trees to the Buckinghams' house about 250 yards away. Grandpa often went there to watch the children playing. He always knew when the Buckingham children were at home, whether he could see them or not. When they were there the house seemed to have an aura about it. No one but Grandpa could sense it.

Julie went with him, holding his hand. She loved to walk beside Grandpa holding his hand. Grandpa was nice. His hand was knobbly, his face was all withered like a dry parsnip and he walked funny. His legs were so far apart that Julie had sometimes thought of running between them.

Julie wasn't quite sure what Grandpa was, except that he wasn't people. She hadn't got round to solving the problems of old age, but she knew that he was never angry like people, and was happy to sit and play when people wouldn't, and told wonderful stories about billy-goats and little pigs and big bad wolves and Pooh Bear and Heffalumps. She used to get God and Grandpa mixed up.

"Well," said Grandpa, viewing the distant and apparently deserted house, "Stevie hasn't found Pippa yet, by the look of it."

Julie had a lot to say about that because Julie had a lot to say about everything, but Grandpa didn't really near her, though he had a remarkable talent for making the right sort of noise when she asked a question. It was sufficient for Grandpa's well-being just to know that she was there, just to feel the pressure of her small hand, just to think his own thoughts against the background tinkle of her almost unceasing chatter. He had addressed himself rather than Julie, though he was not in the least anxious about the absence of the two children. Grandpa wasn't in a fizz about the fire as a lot of people seemed to be. All this talk of evacuation was a lot of nonsense; certainly it was all right for the able-bodied to go out and give others a hand, but he considered it the height of folly for able-bodied people, men or women, to leave their homes in the path of the fire, whether they left of their own accord or not. It was the privilege of the householder to protect his own home.

They'd never shift Grandpa. They'd have to blast him out first.

And as for the fire reaching Ash Road, or Prescott for that matter, Grandpa had never heard nonsense like it. The authorities were talking themselves into a crisis. A bad fire in midsummer was always a serious business, but people were behaving as if a fire had never happened before. Grandpa had reached the point of switching his radio off in disgust; though almost reluctantly he had straightaway switched it on again. Every station was the same. Hysteria. Radio reporters broadcasting from vantage points, from aeroplanes, and from "advanced positions at the scene of the fire". And thousands of volunteers from the city were swarming into the hills to add to the confusion; hundreds of policemen and soldiers and all sorts of people who didn't know one end of a bushfire from the other. They'd end up with a disaster all right, but it was one they would create for themselves. Fighting fires was a job for experts, for bushmen, for cool heads. They were turning it into a glorified picnic, into a holiday of fear and foolishness.

Don Buckingham, in his own way, was just as bad. Gallivanting off to Miltondale. Robertson, too; just as bad. A man's place was with his family, unless he could contribute knowledge and skill to the job on hand. Neither Buckingham nor Robertson knew the first thing about fire-fighting. And that was what was happening. Hundreds of Buckinghams and Robertsons and, worse still, hundreds of inexperienced youths were rushing in where angels would fear to tread.

Grandpa had a suspicion that his thoughts were beginning to

argue back and forth, that perhaps he was a little anxious for the children, that perhaps the fire *could* come. After all, it had come before in his own lifetime. But surely that was different. Surely circumstances had been different in the old days, even the country had been different then. Anyway, Prescott was filling up with evacuees; there was no talk of evacuating Prescott itself. That was why he had Julie with him and the Robertsons' baby in his house. Grandpa smiled when he thought of the baby. That young Mrs Robertson had entrusted her baby to him without the slightest hesitation pleased him tremendously.

He became aware of Julie again, tugging hard on his hand. "Look, look, look, Grandpa," she was saying. "Look at the helipopter!"

The strident beat of its engine blared suddenly on the wind and it turned, almost like a crab, several hundred feet overhead. Grandpa saw, too, in a moment of some concern, that it crabbed round, not against a background of blue sky, but against an immense buff-coloured cloud.

It was smoke.

7. Siberia

GRAMPS FAIRHALL thought for one brief moment of exquisite but incredulous relief that the engine of his car had started firing of its own accord. He had got to the stage where fact and fancy were beginning to merge, but he knew that that sort of thing happened only in dreams. His car was as stubbornly silent as ever. The sound had come from a cursed helicopter beating somewhere overhead.

He leant against the side of his car, panting, trembling, and sweating as he strained to nudge a brick into position behind a front wheel with his foot. He was frustrated, angry, breathless. He hadn't worked so hard in years, and he was determined, absolutely determined, that the car would not beat him. He'd get it up to the road if it killed him.

He couldn't see the helicopter; he could never see very far without his glasses. The distance was always invisible and the middle distance was a fog. In fact Gramps rarely actually saw a helicopter or an aircraft in the air; he knew them only by the sound they made, and there was about that sound up there an urgent and fretful note. He did not like the sound; it shouldn't have been there. The fire had not crossed the crest of the ranges; or so he believed. He knew of no reason why

the helicopter should be there. Gramps did not care much for
mysteries at any time, and at this moment less than usual. What
was that blithering helicopter doing?

He got the brick in position and collapsed against the side of
the car, listening to the sound toss about on the wind, worried
by it, deeply worried. Oh, he didn't like this day. It was a bad
day, an ominous day; his bones ached with fatigue and foreboding.

"Go away," he bellowed at the sky, and obediently the sound
went away. So completely did it dissolve into the roar of the
trees that he wondered whether he had heard it at all, wondered
whether it was something inside him, perhaps his protesting
heart.

He had cranked his car until he couldn't crank it any more,
then with one hand to the steering-wheel and the other clamped
like a flushed and fleshy vice to the car door, he had started
heaving and pushing the obstinate vehicle up the gentle but
long slope from the car-shelter to the road. He was a big man
with the brute strength of sheer bulk, but he was scared to push
too hard, scared to give it everything he had, particularly after
he had caught sight of a face in the rear-vision mirror. It was
his own face and it was contorted and almost purple. It had
given him a terrible fright. If he had not known that his heart
was reasonably sound he would have sworn that he was about
to drop dead. Yet he had pushed on, holding back the last
measure of absolute effort. He had to live long enough to get
the car going, to find Peter, and to get him out of these hills.
By now the boy's parents would be frantic.

He knew, of course, that he should have insisted upon en-
listing the aid of Buckingham and Robertson and the others.
That truckload of men could have pushed the car to the road
in a minute. He was a fool not to have stated his case in more
positive terms, a fool to have let them go. Once his car was on
the road he could coast downhill; then, sooner or later, the
engine would have to fire. But Robertson had been obsessed by
a single thought: to fill his truck with able-bodied men and rush
to Miltondale. Gramps at least had stopped him on the road,
but it hadn't got him anywhere. "OK, Mr Fairhall," Robertson
had called, leaning out, "I wouldn't say, exactly, that it was a

job for you, but hop on and dig your claws in or you'll be shaken off."

"No, no," Gramps had puffed, "I'm too old for that sort of thing. I want some help. I want my car pushed up to the road."

"You want *what?*"

This question had hurt Gramps deeply, for it had been followed by an unnecessarily fierce take-off, by a roar of the truck's engine, and by rear wheels spinning in the gravel, spraying stones like shrapnel. Gramps would never forget that. Robertson could rot before Gramps would buy another bag of coke or another gallon of fuel from him!

He started pushing again, lurching rhythmically against the car to rock it off the brick; then he started heaving again, creeping it up the beastly slope an inch at a time until he had advanced it another couple of yards. Then he pushed the brick into position again and collapsed again and started cursing Peter breathlessly because Peter was not there. Even a boy would have made a difference, that little bit extra, that critical difference between a solitary ordeal and a team effort.

Peter's behaviour was thoughtless, selfish, rebellious, and grossly disobedient. Gramps was furious about it. He had almost resolved to put the boy across his knee and spank him— if there was any strength left in him for so vigorous an exercise. Then he noticed that the light had changed.

Perhaps he had been aware of it, subconsciously, for a minute or two, but had been too fatigued to see it. Shadows had softened. Grass and foliage, even green foliage, had taken on an orange hue. The light was diffused; the whole world about him was flushed as though seen through tinted spectacles.

Gramps stood up straight, his sweaty hands pressed into his back. There was a spasm of pain in his back and a spasm of a different kind in his heart, his mind, his whole awareness. A great body of smoke, high up, must have passed between the earth and the sun. Despite the intense and oppressive heat, Gramps shivered.

It was bad; very bad indeed.

He was frightened, too, for though he had seen a fire or two in his time, he had not seen one here, not a real one, in his own neck of the woods. There were always two kinds of fire—the fire that didn't matter because it was somewhere else, and the other kind, the kind that did matter.

He walked out to the road, unthinkingly, gripped by the irrational feeling that if fire were to come at all it would come along the road, just as everything else that came to him came along the road. He couldn't see anything that looked like fire, couldn't hear anything that sounded like it, and he wished the long hill were not there, would miraculously sink into the earth before his eyes and reveal however indistinctly, what lay beyond it. But the hill remained immovable. It was like a high wall that shut him in, or cut him off, or perhaps stood as a fortress that might repulse the enemy on the other side.

He took a deep breath and bellowed, "Peter! *Peter!*"

Peter didn't answer, didn't appear, but over the crest of the long hill came a vehicle that stopped farther up at Grandpa Tanner's gate. It was the milkman.

They carried Lorna's father to the car in the shed and lifted him on to the back seat.

It was incredibly difficult, for although old man George was wiry rather than heavy they were afraid to rough-handle him; his body felt so unnatural. He was so stiff, so unbending. Even the sound of the helicopter failed to break through to them with meaning. Although it was less than half a mile from them, they were conscious of it only as another noise in a world full of noise, a world that blustered and groaned, and slapped and swirled with the dust of the paddocks; yet a world dominated by the face and body of a silent man. Pippa was afraid that he was as good as dead already and that the curious manifestation of life in his face was an illusion. She had never before understood death in relation to people; she had never seen death; she was horribly afraid that she was about to confront it. Harry thought the man had had a stroke, but was sure he had read somewhere that the symptoms were different. Wallace was merely frightened, tense, and awfully weak, for anything that was not normal always unnerved him. Stevie was pop-eyed, as if witnessing an event that didn't belong to his own world; he trembled all over and bitterly regretted his eager offer to show

Wallace the way to the hospital. He didn't want to be in the same car as this strange creature that not so long ago he had known as old man George. Lorna just didn't know what was wrong with him and didn't want to discuss it, anyway. She didn't want to distress her father—because his hearing might have been unimpaired—and she didn't want to add to her own .error.

When they had got him onto the back seat they were afraid he would fall off, and Harry had to sit against him to make sure that he wouldn't, and Lorna said to Wallace, "I'll come. I'll show you the way. It's my place to go with him."

"Well, you'd better clean yourself up," said Pippa. "You can't go like that."

"Like what?"

"Oh, Lorna. You ought to see yourself."

"What's wrong with me?" said Lorna, looking at her hands and at her clothes. She sighed. "What does it matter, Pippa? It's so unimportant."

Wallace walked around the car a couple of times, with Stevie on his heels. There wasn't much room, for the shed was full of tools and sacks and empty cases. "It's a bloomin' awful old car," Stevie said. "It's older than I am."

"Yeh," grunted Wallace. "Older than me, too."

There were a couple of chocks under the front wheels. Perhaps this meant that the brakes were not too good. "What are the brakes like?" Wallace called to Lorna.

"You've got to pump them. Is that the word?"

"Yeh," said Wallace, "I thought so.

He slid into the driver's seat and was confronted by a strange set of instruments that meant nothing to him at all. "English," he said heavily.

"Yes."

"I knew it," he groaned. "That means the gears'll be different, too."

"I'll stick here," said Harry to Lorna, "to make sure he doesn't fall off. You sit in the front with Wallace."

Pippa and Stevie drew away to a safe distance (the farther away the better as far as Stevie was concerned, in case Lorna changed her mind and asked him to go instead), and Wallace fiddled with the gears until he got them in neutral. "How d'you start the bloomin' thing?" he said.

"I don't know," said Lorna, "except that Dad presses a button, I think."

"What button?" said Wallace.

Lorna sat beside him and slammed the door and pointed. "One of those, I think. He turns it on and then presses it."

"Can't turn it on without the key," said Wallace. "Where's the key?"

"Oh dear . . . I don't know."

"Crumbs," said Wallace. "You'd better find it then. We won't get anywhere without it."

Lorna suddenly felt helpless again and sick with disappointment. "I don't know where he keeps it."

"Well you'd better look."

"What's the good? I don't know where to look. I don't think I've ever seen the key about the house. Ever."

Harry said, "When did he use it last?"

"Sunday."

"He hasn't used it for a *week?*"

"John goes in on his motor bike to do the shopping. He's got bags on the pillion seat to put things in."

"John's your brother?"

Lorna nodded.

"Well, where did your dad go in the car?" Harry asked.

"To church."

"All right then. Look in the pockets of his Sunday suit."

"They're not in his suit. I know they're not. I always press his suit. There are never any keys in it."

"Strike me," said Harry. "You're making it hard."

"It's not me," said Lorna thickly. "Dad's so secretive about some things. There are lots of things I wouldn't know where to find if I had to . . . ."

Harry looked into the face of the man he held. "We tried, sir," he said, "but there's nothing we can do about this lot, unless you can tell us where the ignition key is."

"It's like a nightmare," Lorna whispered. "Nothing goes right."

Pippa came back to the door of the car, and they told her

what was wrong. Tears ran down Lorna's face. "I don't know where it is," she said. "And he can't tell us. It's not fair. It's not fair . . . ."

"Well, surely we can look for it," said Pippa. "It's got to be somewhere."

"What's the use?" Lorna cried. "He hides things."

Suddenly Stevie shrieked, "I can hear a car! A car!"

"Well stop it!" they yelled together.

Pippa took off after Stevie, and Wallace floundered out of the front seat into a crashing confusion of tool handles and collapsing stacks of empty wooden boxes; by the time he had fought his way out of them, fuming and shouting, Pippa and Stevie were out of sight.

They glimpsed the car, the tail-end of it, a utility truck pulling away from the gateway.

"The milkman!"

They ran like mad, yelling and shrieking into the wind, waving their arms. The driver didn't notice them. He had arrived unheard, left the milk bottles in the box, turned and pulled away again, up the hill. Stevie had heard him driving off.

They reached the road, still yelling, still waving their arms, but the milkman had gone beyond call. The Georges' box was his last stop that morning on Ash Road, and now he was heading back to Prescott or somewhere else. They didn't know where. They didn't know which route he took.

"Oh, Stevie," panted Pippa. "Poor Lorna."

Wallace arrived limping. Lorna had stopped halfway down the path, too dispirited to come any farther.

"That's that," said Wallace. "You can be stiff, can't you?"

"The baker doesn't come today, either," said Stevie.

"Who does come?" said Wallace. "Anybody?"

"Not on Saturdays."

"Gosh. Talk about Siberia."

"Well, I reckon someone will have to walk," said Pippa. "We've got legs. It's silly standing round doing nothing. And I reckon someone should get back on that phone and start ringing everybody for miles around until someone answers. Someone's got to be at home. It's just plain silly. And I reckon someone should walk up to the highway and stop the first car that comes by."

"How far is it to the highway?" said Wallace.

"Two miles."

"Crikey. Two more miles'd kill me. Me feet are like dirty great lumps o' meat."

"I'll go," said Stevie.

"You're too little. You've got to stop with me."

"I'm not too little. I'll be in the fifth grade this year, and I wasn't too little to come lookin' for you."

"You're stopping with me," said Pippa firmly. "I'm responsible for you."

"Aw," said Stevie.

"It's a bad day. It's dangerous. Just look at the light and the smoke up there."

To tell the truth it was the first time Pippa had noticed it herself. It was a sudden revelation, an awakening, a shock.

"Golly," breathed Pippa. "Just look at it."

"Yeh," said Wallace. "And it's rainin' ash if you please."

Ash was eddying on the wind like snowflakes, fragments of burnt fern fronds, pieces of charred leaves. Probably it had blown for miles. The sky was full of it.

8. Gramps

"Does it mean the fire's comin'?" Stevie said. "It's awful-lookin', isn't it? T'isn't like a fire at all."

Pippa turned a frown on him. "If you do see it, you'll like it even less. Fire that'll put up smoke like that isn't the sort you want to see." Not that Pippa wanted to see either.

Stevie squinted again into the sky. The smoke cloud was a pale brown overcast with billows of white and curious areas of mahogany and streaks of sulphurous-looking yellow. The sun shone through like a white plate in a bowl full of dye, but the light on the road was reddish. There was ash on the road, too, unnumbered flakes of it lying in the gravel and in the grass at the edges and caught up like black flowers in twigs and foliage. They turned to powder when Stevie touched them.

"I say," said Wallace, almost unbelievingly, "isn't that the milkman coming back again?" He wondered how it could be the milkman coming into sight over the same hump in the road over which he had disappeared; but who else could it be?

Pippa yelled for Lorna. "A car. Quick. Quick." She pushed Stevie. "Run, Stevie. Make sure he sees you. He might turn round or something."

Stevie ran, and the others waved their arms and jumped and shouted, and Lorna arrived, half-laughing, half-crying. "It's the Fairhalls, Pippa," she shrieked. "It's the Fairhalls' car. It is. It is."

Stevie, floundering up the hill, also recognized it as the Fairhalls' car. Finally out of breath, he reeled to the side of the road and waited for it. It came lurching and shuddering towards the boy, blowing clouds of exhaust smoke, roaring and coughing, and then stopped a couple of hundred yards short of him, its engine beating at a high rate of revolutions. Stevie realized with dismay, that Gramps Fairhall couldn't see him, or was ignoring him, or was so preoccupied that he wasn't even looking.

"Mr Fairhall," he shouted and started running again, with Pippa and Lorna after him.

"Mr Fairhall! Mr Fairhall!"

Stevie got there first and grabbed at the door handle and anchored himself to it as if to prevent its escape.

"Mr Fairhall," he panted, and an enormous, florid face, bereft of hair except for two bushy eyebrows, demanded, "What are you doing here, young Buckingham? I thought you were with your mother. Have you got Peter with you? . . . What's that you say?"

Gramps seemed incapable of realizing that Stevie didn't have the breath to make himself heard above the engine.

"What was that about Peter?" he demanded a second time. "What did you say?"

Pippa and Lorna arrived, flushed and breathless, throats so dry they could scarcely make a sound.

"What are you children doing, running around on a day like this?" Gramps boomed. "Where's Peter?"

"Oh, Mr Fairhall," gasped Lorna, "my dad's sick. He's dying, I think. You've got to take him to hospital. Please, Mr Fairhall, please."

"Can't hear you, child. Speak up."

"Switch the engine off," yelled Pippa.

"Can't," boomed Gramps. "Got to charge my battery. If I stop it, it mightn't start again. Tell Peter to come here at once or I'll tan the hide off him."

"Mr Fairhall," cried Lorna. "It's my father. He's ill. Terribly ill."

"Peter ill? What do you mean, Peter ill?"

"Not Peter," shrieked Lorna hysterically. "My dad. My dad!

Oh goodness, what's wrong with everybody? Isn't *anybody* going to help me?"

"Bless my soul," boomed Gramps, "you'd better get a grip on yourself, young lady. It's your father that's ill, is it? Well why did you say it was Peter?"

"She didn't," screamed Pippa. "Do switch that stupid engine off. Do stop roaring it!"

Gramps frowned irritably and eased his foot off a little. "If this engine stops," he barked, "you'll have to push until it starts again. I've had troubles enough for one morning. I've got to get Peter back to town before all the roads are closed. You tell Peter to come here at once."

"Please, Mr Fairhall," pleaded Pippa, "Lorna's dad is very, very sick. He's paralysed. He's got to be taken to hospital. Can't you take him?"

Gramps drew his bushy eyebrows together, still with a trace of irritation. "If Mr George is sick, surely the doctor can get an ambulance?"

"Lorna can't get an ambulance, can't even get a doctor. She can't get anybody."

"He can't be too sick, then."

"But he is, Mr Fairhall. Really and truly, he's terribly sick. He looks like a dead man. She's been trying to get help for ages. She's so cut off."

Gramps grunted. "I don't know what I can do."

"You can take him, can't you?"

"If he's paralysed as you say," said Gramps, "how do I get him to the car? I can't take the car to him. I mustn't run it down the Georges' driveway. If it stops I'll never get it out again."

"Please," appealed Lorna, almost hopelessly. "Could you come to the head of the drive then, and leave the rest to us?"

"Well where's Peter? I can't go without Peter. Is he with you?"

"Peter's in the bush," squealed Stevie. "That's where he is. Hiding."

"Well turf him out for me, young fellow. You bring him here."

"Gee whiz," said Stevie, "I don't know about that. How

d'you find a fella when he's hidin'?"

"Look for him," boomed Gramps. "It's as simple as that . . . . all right, you kids. Hop in the back. I'll run you down to the gate."

They scrambled in. Lorna was crying to herself and Gramps said, "Has your dad been working in the paddock this morning?"

"Yes, sir."

"More fool him. A man of his age out in heat like this. And up half the night, I suppose, shifting those blithering sprinklers?"

"Yes, sir," said Lorna.

Gramps snorted and jolted off down the hill. "Fire's bad," he said. "It's over the top, they tell me. In the pine forest. I was speaking to the milkman. Tearing hurry he was in, too. Right along the top, he said, on a front of about ten miles. Three hundred houses, he said, razed to the ground. You young Buckinghams had better come back with me. I'll drop you off at your house. That's where you ought to be, sitting at that telephone. Your father needs his head read, rushing off and leaving you to yourselves on a day like this."

He stopped opposite the Georges' gateway. "All right. Pile out. I'll turn her round and wait. And you, young Stevie, find Peter! No excuses. Find him. Until you find him I don't budge from here."

"But he might have gone home again by now," wailed Stevie.

"Not him. Flattens m'battery for me and leaves me to push the car to the road. If it hadn't been for the milkman I'd still be there."

Pippa and Lorna stumbled down the drive. They were past running. They were both wrung out. "The boys have gone," sobbed Lorna. "I just know they've gone. No sign of them."

Pippa was afraid of that, too. It was the sort of thing that would happen. The first one had vanished at the earliest opportunity, and that was before the other two had blurted out their story. She knew they'd be gone. Anything else was too much to hope for. But she said, "Don't be silly. They wouldn't do that."

"Everybody else has."

"Mr Fairhall hasn't."

"Only because he couldn't get out of it. Only because it suits him, anyway, because he's got to take Peter."

The boys were in the shed. They had Lorna's father out of the car and back on to the door they had used as a stretcher. When Lorna saw them she could no longer stifle her crying, and Pippa had to comfort her. The boys looked away, and to Pippa it was all like a bad dream. She felt she'd have to be kind to Lorna, to stick to her for ever and always, for as long as she lived.

Stevie rushed down the road towards the bend, yelling for Peter. "Peter Fairhall, you stinker. Where are you, Peter Fairhall?"

Then he rushed up again. "If you don't show your ugly mug, Peter Fairhall, I'll kick your teeth in."

Then he rushed down again, round the bend. "Please, Peter. Please. Come on out. Be a sport."

Then he picked up a handful of stones and threw them fiercely in the bush. "You're a louse, Fairhall. That's what you are. G'arn. I bet you're not even game to come out and fight."

Then he reached the gate to Hobson's place, where the apples grew. "If you're eatin' apples, Fairhall, I hope they give you a belly-ache."

Then he got tired and discouraged and climbed over the gate because there was a lock on it, and picked an apple for himself. It was as green as grass and he spat it out.

Then he climbed back over the gate and plodded up the hill again towards the bend, muttering to himself.

The four young people arrived at the roadside bearing old man George on the door, and placed him gently on the ground near the rear end of the car. Gramps, still with one foot to the accelerator, leant out and took a look. He took a long look, first at his neighbour, then at his neighbour's bedraggled daughter. Poor kid. She looked done in. Gramps suddenly felt profoundly ashamed of himself. Probably there was no real need for shame, but he felt it, not so much because he had been impatient with the children as because this tired old man on the ground had obviously all but worked himself to death, just as Gramps would have had to do if he had not had his secret inheritance. He had often told old man George that he had retired in comfort on the profits of a well-run farm, but only in one bumper year had his farm ever made better than wages. And old George had done this to himself to keep a disgruntled, complaining, whining woman in the comfort of a private ward of a rest home!

"Can you get him up all right? Can you get him in?"

"Yes, sir," said Harry.

Gramps turned a keen eye on the lad and then on Wallace. "Who are you?" he said. "Where'd you come from?"

"They're friends of the Pinkards," said Pippa quickly. "They've been trying to help us. They were going to drive the old car for us, but we couldn't find the key."

"All right. Get him in . . . . Now where's Stevie with that Peter?" But Gramp's concern for Peter had undergone a change. If all these kids were mucking in, helping the Georges, why wasn't Peter? Hiding, indeed. What was he hiding for? He felt a pang of guilt about Peter. The boy was a bit of a namby-pamby.

The car lurched to the weight of the two lads as they struggled in through the rear door with the sick man, and in a moment of acute vision Gramps confronted the face of old man George at a distance of about eighteen inches. Gramps had to look away, had to turn back to the front, for he had seen more than a moment of pain; he had looked straight into a lifetime of disappointment and defeat.

"I'll have to come with you, I think, sir," said Harry, "to hold him, or he'll fall off the seat."

"If you think so, lad."

"Me, too, sir," said Wallace.

"Why, lad? There are others to fit in, you know."

Wallace felt that it was very important to stay with Harry. He felt inadequate by himself. Harry seemed to understand things, to know what he was doing. "I thought, maybe," said Wallace, "that after we'd got to the hospital you could drop us both off somewhere, at a fire station maybe. I reckon they must need all the help they can get."

"Yes," said Gramps, "yes . . . . That's the right kind of idea. Hop in, lad . . . ." He turned to Lorna again and the gentleness, the concern for her that was in him broke through to her. "Lorna, dear," he said, "you're not going to achieve anything by coming with your dad. You go inside and lie down. By the look of you, you've had more than you can stand. You've got your telephone. We'll keep in touch. If you're needed, we'll let you know. Don't worry about that. Don't worry about anything. Your dad'll soon be in good hands."

Lorna didn't make a move one way or the other. She felt she couldn't turn away, yet she dreaded climbing into the car.

"Later on," said Gramps, "when Mrs Fairhall gets back from Prescott, she'll come down to you. We'll leave a note for her. There's a good girl. What do you say?"

Pippa squeezed her arm. "Go on, Lorna. You go and lie down. You'll feel better in no time, and I'll see if I can trace John. We can do it on the phone. I'll stay with you till Mrs Fairhall comes."

"You know you've got to go home," said Lorna miserably. "There are all those things your mother wants you to do, and you haven't had any breakfast. I heard Stevie say so."

"My mother won't mind when she knows what's happened to you. And I can have some breakfast with you."

"All right," Lorna said. She leant into the car and kissed her father, and then ran away, back down the drive. Pippa for the moment was caught flat-footed. Gramps found her eye. "Off you go, lass. Stick with her. And make sure she rests."

Pippa fell back a couple of paces, then turned and went after Lorna.

Gramps said to Wallace, "Can you see that grandson of mine? Is he coming?"

"No, sir," said Wallace. "Not a soul in sight; not even the little kid you sent after him."

Gramps reached firmly towards a decision. In all honesty, wasn't Peter's plight imaginary? In all honesty, wasn't the fire, no matter how bad it looked, a long way beyond that impassable barrier of water, the dam? Even if by some strange chance it did reach Ash Road it would not be for many hours, probably for days. Probably never. But old man George's plight was not imaginary.

When Stevie trudged round the lower bend a minute or two later the road was deserted.

He stopped, hands on hips, swaying. "How's their rotten form?" he squealed to the wind. "Left me for dead. Now I've got to *walk* home."

9. The Angry Day

PETER wondered what time it was. It was not something he had to know; it was only part of his restlessness and anxiety. He didn't know whether it was seven o'clock or eight o'clock or later. The summer sun was deceptive. It was so high in the sky so soon in the day.

It was hard to say exactly what thought was uppermost in Peter's mind, for he was unable to concentrate on any one thing long enough. He knew he had to go home to Gramps but the longer he delayed the act the harder the decision to move off became. He feared the consequences of his break with Pippa but was reluctant to try to mend it in case the rift became worse. He knew it was not yet ten-thirty, when the Buckinghams would leave for Deer Sands—if they were to go at all— so the point of urgency when he *had* to find Pippa had not arrived. He was suspicious of the intentions of the unknown boy hiding somewhere in the bush behind him but didn't have the courage to turn back to face him. Facing people was much harder than following them. And he was frightened of the sky. It was so threatening, so ugly, so unlike anything he had ever seen. It was a hot brown mantle over the earth with pieces breaking off it, little black pieces of ash; an oppressive mantle that did not prevent the penetration of the sun's heat but imprisoned it, added to it, and magnified the hostility of the day.

It was an angry day; not just wild or rough, but savage in itself, actively angry against every living thing. It hated plants and trees and birds and animals, and they wilted from its hatred or withered up and died or panted in distress in shady places. Above all, it hated Peter. It seemed to encompass him with a malevolence that would strike him down if he ventured to defy it. There was a wall around him, an invisible wall that confined him to a few square yards of hot, dusty earth at the bottom of the George's carrot paddock. He longed to burst out, to seek the shade like the birds and other creatures, to drink a long draught of cool water, but he couldn't move.

The day was so angry with him that he was frightened to raise a hand against it.

In the house it was dark behind drawn blinds, and less hot, and Lorna said there was a jug of lemon water chilled in the refrigerator. Pippa had difficulty finding it; there was no light inside the refrigerator and everything was so gloomy. When she flicked the switch on the wall the light in the ceiling didn't come on, either. Eventually she took a glass of lemon water into Lorna's bedroom and said, "Do you want this, or would you rather have tea?"

Lorna drank the lemon water.

"What about breakfast?" said Pippa. "Have you had any yourself?"

Lorna nodded.

"What about a plate of cornflakes or something?"

"No. But if you cook something I'll eat it with you to keep you company."

"You're to stay where you are—unless you want to take a bath."

Lorna smiled wanly. "You mean I should take a bath?"

"It's bound to help you pull yourself together. Particularly if it's a warm one."

"I suppose so." Lorna lowered her feet from the bed to the floor. "Perhaps I will, and change my clothes."

"Yes," said Pippa. "I'll run it for you."

"It's a kerosene heater, Pippa. It's so slow and makes a dreadful noise. It's not like yours."

"I'll manage."

"I'd rather do it myself. You might blow the place up. And I'd rather you tried to get a message through to John."

"Yes," said Pippa. "I'll do it now."

"Do have your breakfast first."

"Don't be silly. I wouldn't dream of it."

"You're very good, Pippa."

"Don't say that. I don't feel good at all."

Talking wasn't easy. It would have been better not to have tried. They had gone through a raw time together and hadn't got over it. Lorna was nerve-racked and weak. It was too soon to forget the desperation and the pain: much too soon. She felt as if her soul had been stripped in front of Pippa, and she was still embarrassed, still faintly humiliated. For Pippa, though a friend, was not an intimate friend. Lorna had not an intimate friend in the whole world. She needed time to get her dignity back, time for the aches of her heart and head and body to heal a little, to be washed over by fresh events. And Pippa, with unusual intuition, all but guessed the state of Lorna's mind. Indeed, she needed time herself to recover from the bewilderment of confronting, for the first time in her life, a fellow human-being in an hour of cruel crisis. Anguish had never touched Pippa's life before. It shocked her.

"I'll ring the fire brigade first," Pippa said. "And if they don't answer I might try the vicar."

"Oh," said Lorna.

"What is it?"

"I should have thought of the vicar before."

"Goodness. I don't know how you thought of everything that you did think of."

Pippa went into the living-room to the telephone, and Lorna walked slowly to the bathroom. The matches had apparently fallen from the window sill above the water-heater and dropped in the gloom behind the bath. And the light wouldn't come on. She flicked the switch up and down several times, uselessly. She thought the globe had burnt out until she tried the switch in the passage outside. The passage light didn't work either.

And when Pippa picked up the telephone it was dead; quite dead. No matter how often she tried she could not produce the dial tone.

She heard Lorna behind her. "It won't work, will it?"

"No . . . ."

"It's my fault. I should have made sure before I let Mr Fairhall go."

"Oh, Lorna. How can you blame yourself for that?"

"The power's off, too."

"I know . . . ."

"It's not my day, is it?"

Pippa didn't know what to say. Lorna sat heavily in a deep, leather-backed chair and closed her eyes. Her face was that of a grubby little girl. She looked about eight years of age.

"Oh, Pippa. It isn't fair . . . ."

The boys didn't know that Gramps was short-sighted. They assumed that the spectacle of the inferno along the crest of the ranges failed to excite his comment because it was less serious than it looked—though it looked serious enough, Heaven knew. As soon as the car breasted the top of the long hill the horizon of the fire boiled into their vision. Smoke boomed from the horizon. The earth seemed to have split for miles along the ridge of the range, allowing vast reservoirs of smoke and flame, long trapped beneath the surface, to come gushing out. It was an explosion, a continuing explosion of unimaginable violence, of dark and fierce turbulence. It seemed inconceivable that any living thing or any structure built by man could survive within it. It seemed that it must melt the earth.

Wallace turned and found Harry's eyes. Harry's eyes were wide; appalled, unbelieving. They said to Wallace, "Did we start this? This *can't* be our doing!" If Harry had spoken the words Wallace could not have heard them more clearly. But Gramps Fairhall didn't express surprise or the vaguest concern; he merely kept his eyes on the road ahead, plodding on at a steady thirty-five miles an hour, avoiding the more obvious debris peeled by the high wind from the trees by the roadside. He came to the crossroads, past the potato paddock lying fallow, and turned west towards Prescott. The signpost said, *Prescott 2 miles.*

"He doesn't seem worried," Harry said to himself. "It can't be as bad as it looks."

And Wallace said to himself, "Blowed if I know, but he's a cool customer."

Down in the dip, about a mile and a half from the township, Gramps stopped the car short of a tree lying across the road. They had come upon it suddenly, round a bend. It was an old blackwood, a giant, rotten at the butt from the ravages of beetles and grubs, that had borne to the road a horizontal mass of fractured boughs and branches and foliage more than twenty feet high. It would have taken a dozen men with axes and saws an hour to clear it away.

Gramps grunted. "We'll have to go round by the highway. There's no other way."

He turned and drove back to Ash Road, then headed northwards again, towards the source of the unspeakably horrid sky, round Ash Road's curves, past the deserted acres of James Collins and Sons, the nurserymen, until the highway intersected the old road and cut it off at Bill Robertson's corner. There another signpost declared that it was still two miles to Prescott. The looming, tortured mountains seemed very close. Beyond the grey and wind-whipped surface of the dam the dark-green forest climbed towards the smoke, and closer, much closer to them, a line of cars packed with women and children and household items crawled in the direction of Prescott. And barring Gramps's further progress was a barrier across the road, a barrier he had never seen before. "What blithering impertinence is this?" he bellowed.

He stopped, because he could not drive through it and was not at all sure that he could drive round it.

"Ridiculous," he barked. "And what are all these people jamming the road for? They'd do better to go the other way, towards the city."

"It looks as if there's a notice on the barrier, sir," said Wallace.

"Well, take a look at it."

Wallace jumped out and walked round to the other side. "It

says 'No Through Road'," he yelled.

"All right! Drag it across a few feet. Give me room to get past."

"Do you think you should, sir?"

Gramps turned crimson. "I'll do as I think fit!"

Wallace dragged it across, and Gramps drove through. "Will I put it back again, sir?" Wallace asked.

"Put it back? No blithering fear. Leave it where it is. They can't close the road to its residents. Hop in."

Wallace hopped in, and Gramps cut into the traffic stream, but once in it he knew he couldn't accelerate through it. The highway was the only road that was open, and he had to take it at a crawl whether he liked it or not, along with everyone else. He fretted to break out of it, to form a second lane and pass, but it was too risky. It was a highway in name only; the road wasn't wide enough, except in the final approach to Prescott. But there he couldn't pass, either; police directed the traffic, turning it all to the left, into the heart of the town, and Gramps wanted to go to the right. He jammed his feet on the brake and stayed put in the middle of the intersection, and when the policeman shouted at him he shouted back, and Wallace and Harry longed to shrink into invisibility. For this was not like the lonely bush only a few miles away; it was a world of houses and people and car engines and voices and groups of staring people. Here were vehicles drawn up by the roadside near a service station, vehicles bearing drums of water and knapsack sprays and piles of wet hessian and dozens of noisy young men. And farther down Main Street, in the town, were more parked vehicles heaped with furniture and television sets and baby carriages and bedding. Down there, too, were crowds of people wandering without purpose or intent, people down from the mountains, wondering what had happened to them, wondering whether their homes still stood or were heaps of ashes and tangled iron, people bewildered by the catastrophe that had so rapidly overtaken them. For they could still see their mountains, at the opposite end of Main Street, dark mountains in the shadow of dense smoke, mountains that sometimes erupted isolated towers ˜of flame far away, flame so brilliant that it seared through smoke and gloom with the violence of a cannon in the night.

"You!" roared the policemen. "Go left. Left! That way!"

"Miltondale," boomed Gramps. "I'm going to Miltondale."

"Go that way," roared the policeman.

"Miltondale," boomed Gramps.

The policeman strode to the car. He was a young man, a stranger in town. Gramps had never seen him before.

"Do as you're told," shouted the policeman.

"I'm not out for a joy-ride," boomed Gramps. "I've got a dying man on the back seat. Look for yourself. And if I don't get him to hospital, he *will* be dead!"

"You can't go to Miltondale. The road's closed. I've got my orders. The road's closed, except to authorized and incoming traffic. Turn left. You're holding everybody up."

"Listen to me," growled Gramps. "This is my town. It's been my town for more than forty years. It was my town before you knew your right hand from your left. If I want to go right, I go right."

He let in the clutch fiercely and leapt across the intersection, dislodging the startled policeman by force. Then he put his foot down and left Prescott behind. "Fasten your safety belts," he said.

It was five miles to Miltondale, through the populated gullies and along the creek road and through the State Forest where no one lived.

Stevie trudged through the gate, sweating profusely and swearing to himself.

Stevie didn't swear much. He knew two or three words that he mistakenly believed to be terribly wicked, and when he was really mad with the world or its inhabitants he muttered them over and over again, taking great care that no grown-up overheard him. After all, he was rarely so mad with the world that he wanted to suffer for it.

He plodded round the house, too tired even to swing a kick at the invitation of an empty can, banged through the screen door, and shouted: "I hate you, Pippa Buckingham. Why didn't you wait for me?"

Pippa didn't answer.

"That old Gramps Fairhall is a creep. Sendin' me off for Peter on a wild-goose chase and then not givin' me a ride home. He said he was goin' to give me a ride home."

Pippa didn't answer.

"Where are you? G'arn. Answer me, Pippa!"

The house creaked to the heat and groaned to the wind, and no one answered.

"Don't be mean, Pippa. Where are you?"

Stevie wandered from room to room, a little cautiously, because he thought Pippa might jump out to frighten him. She didn't.

"Gee whiz. She's not here. Where is she? Where's Pippa?"

The only living thing in the house was the cat, and it was asleep, stretched out full length on the foot of Julie's bed.

"Where's she gone?"

He returned to the back step and yelled her name across the garden. There was nothing out there either, except the carpets drying in the sun.

He poured himself a glass of ginger beer from a bottle in the refrigerator and took a handful of biscuits from the jar on the pantry shelf and sat down to deal with them.

He didn't mind being on his own when he was outside playing, or down in the gully looking for worms or tadpoles, or running errands, but that wasn't like being alone in an empty house. An empty house was nasty, because it felt empty, surrounded him with emptiness. Emptiness was queer.

What had happened to Pippa? Where had she gone? She was supposed to come home to help him bring the carpets inside and to put water in the spouts and to fill up all the buckets and things and put them round the house and to listen for the telephone and to have breakfast. Pippa was mean.

For the first time the sound of the wind began to worry Stevie. It rattled the windowpanes and scraped the branches of the silver birch tree against the roof and caused all sorts of different noises in all sorts of different places.

"Gee," said Stevie.

There was a wireless on top of the fridge. He switched it on to drown out the other noises. But the dial didn't light up.

"Bloomin' old thing," he said, and started singing to himself, the way his mother did when she was particularly unhappy.

Gramps was stopped twice along the creek road before he reached the State Forest, once by another policeman, once by an army sergeant. To their questions he stated his case bluntly, with suitable epithets directed against those who on any pretext would delay his errand of mercy. It was not only to Peter that Gramps was a menacing character. Something in his bulk, some quality of his immense voice, intimidated people, and each time he was allowed to proceed. At the edge of the forest, where smoke was so low that it swirled through the trees, the army sergeant said, "No one's come through here in twenty minutes. We've had a stream of people from Miltondale and they've stopped coming. It's bound to be risky."

"It's my risk," boomed Gramps.

"What about your passengers?"

Gramps glanced at the boys. "Well?" he said.

"I've got faith in you, sir," said Harry.

"Yeh," said Wallace.

And they did have. Gramps had impressed them tremendously. They would have driven with him through a brick wall if his continued contempt for visible forms of danger had assured them it was possible. And Gramps was not blind to the danger now. He was not so short-sighted that the gloom and the smoke and the nervousness of other people escaped his attention. He set the nose of his car into the forest and put his foot down with three miles of heaven knew what lying between him and Miltondale.

He roared into the forest with his headlights on and with the speedometer on fifty. He knew every turn of the road like the back of his hand, knew every rise and very dip. He had pushed vehicles along this road for more than forty years; he had driven horse-carts over it when it had been a track full of pot-holes and ridges. More often than not he traversed it in perfect safety without a conscious memory of having observed a single foot of it. That was how he drove now, at a far higher speed than a man of superior vision would have dared, unaware of what passed him by, except gloom and eerie glow and random shafts of sunlight and the gothic arch of the tall timber through which he rushed.

Wallace and Harry were aware of other things; Wallace of the heat, of the smoke-laden air that sometimes made him cough, of the sheer excitement of an apparent race against time, of the dimness ahead and the blur of the road, and of Harry sitting tensely and precariously on the edge of the back seat with the extremities of his safety-belt barely meeting at the clasp, and with his right hand closed over the sick man's shoulder. Harry's feelings went deeper than impressions, they went straight to questions. Why was the road deserted? Why was there smoke without fire? Where was the fire, for the heat was such that it could have been the blast from an oven thrown open? Was it that the fire upwind was so vast and so widespread that heat went everywhere before it like dragon's breath?

Gramps's voice intruded suddenly. "Wind up the windows! Jump to it!"

It was the voice of command, and their hands leapt to obey. Then they saw flames to the right, flames at tree-top height exploding like surf on rocks: waves of flame, torrents of flame, flame spraying in fragments, in thousands of pieces, in flaring leaves and twigs that rained onto the road in a storm of fire. It was upon them in seconds, or they had come upon it so swiftly that there was no turning from it: no time to turn, no chance to turn, no place to turn.

Wallace cried out, not conscious of his voice or of his words, conscious only of the appalling magnitude of what he saw and of what he was certain was about to engulf him. It was as if the sky, aflame, was about to fall and smother him in clouds of fire, yet he sensed beside him the big man with a mouthful of bared teeth shouting things like, "God", "Mother of God", "Hold on, boy", "Courage, boy". And Gramps went into it with his foot to the floor because there was nothing else he could do, and Harry went into it screaming the only prayer that could break through his terror: "Gentle Jesus meek and mild . . . ." The car straddled the centre line; it was the thin white line that Gramps clung to; that rolled and swayed beneath him in excess of sixty miles an hour; that was his anchor to the earth, for everything else was swirling fire and smoke and invisibility and stifling heat, fearful heat, that consumed the very air he breathed. His lungs felt that they would burst, and his senses swam, and the thin white line began to wander and wobble, and he knew he was going to lose it, he knew that it was going to get away from him, and in panic he touched the brakes.

Instantly he lost the line. It vanished. He didn't know whether it had gone to his left or his right, and the smoke was as dense as a fog, and his tyres were squealing, scorching rubber sliding on bitumen. He felt the change from hard surface to loose surface, from sealed surface to the gravel at the side of the road. In that moment the car struck the bank side-on and spun.

Twice more the car struck the bank, first tail on, then head on; then it stopped.

10. Peter

HARRY was stunned. For a time he barely realized that he was alive. Then little by little he began to understand that his safety-belt had held; that Lorna's father, secured to the seat scarcely less awkwardly than he, had changed position but had not been dislodged; and that Wallace and Gramps Fairhall still sat in the front almost as if they had gone to sleep.

Though the fire still roared, there seemed to be an odd silence. The engine of the car had stopped, and the heat was almost unimaginable. What was outside Harry didn't know. All the glass in the car, except one side panel, had cracked, perhaps from the impact, perhaps from the heat. The windscreen was quite opaque, a crazed mass, and the door handles were almost too hot to touch. But Harry had to have air; it didn't matter what sort of air; he had to have it. He snatched at the handle and kicked the door open.

He stumbled to the road into an extraordinary world of blacks and greys and tongues of fire. It was like a black and white photograph of enormous proportions, in the midst of which candles burned mysteriously. It was a creaking and cracking and rending world superimposed upon a thunderous background roar. It was a world of wraiths and ghosts and changing shapes, of fantastic forms fashioned from smoke. It was a world of acrid odours, of strange smells and sensations, terrifyingly unreal, but a world becoming cooler, for the monster had swept over it and gone bellowing into the depths of the forest. It left behind it a hundred thousand tiny fires in the boughs and branches of seared trees and in the undergrowth, thousands of tiny fires that flaked off from the heights and fell through masses of foliage stiff and pale and dehydrated, millions of sparks that scattered on the wind, and legions of tiny dead creatures. Snakes and lizards and feathered creatures and furred creatures were strewn the length of the road or lay buried in the forest ashes.

Harry saw this grotesque world but scarcely comprehended it, for he saw it through a mist. It was a mist of salty tears that welled from his smarting eyes, a mist of coughing and confusion and nausea. He was sick where he stood. He was sick until each contraction of his muscles was like the turn of a knife. Then he stood blankly, unseeing, swaying, swallowing air and smoke and vapours in great gulps, groaning and shuddering in his bones; and suddenly, with startling clarity, questioning whether he alone had survived.

He was not alone. Gramps had Wallace sitting at the side of the road, bending the boy by the trunk, forcing his head between his knees, and all four doors of the car were flung open. The paint on the car was blistered; the rear end, the front end, and one side were partly crushed; and twin tracks of black on the bitumen and sweeping marks in the gravel defined the path the skid had taken.

Gramps said to Harry, "All right now, boy?"

"Yes, sir."

"Close shave, that."

"Yes, sir."

"Better than running from it, though. We'd have fried, for certain."

"Didn't we?"

Gramps shrugged. "Never seen a fire so fast. Thirty miles an hour, I'd say. Just as well it was, boy. Or we'd have fried just the same."

Gramps looked at though he had, partly. His voice, so

confident and possessed, belied his wretched appearance. "Remember that, boy; safest place in a fire is behind it, if you can get there . . . . Here, look after your mate. I'd better see to Mr George."

"Is he dead?"

Gramps looked at him sharply. "What made you say that?"

"I don't know."

"Well, don't talk of death."

Gramps turned to the car, and Harry helped Wallace to his feet. Wallace looked crimson and green at the same time. He shivered in Harry's arms. "Strike me," he stammered. "Oh strike me, strike me."

But Harry was watching Gramps, or the part of him that he could see, his feet to the ground. The rest of him bent over the man on the back seat. Harry tried to read through Gramps's feet what Gramps saw through his eyes.

Then Gramps said, "He's a tough old bird. I thought m'self he'd be dead." Gramps straightened up. He knocked out a hole in the crazed windscreen with his forearm, brushed the pieces away, and resumed his seat. He freed the gears and pressed the starter. The engine fired.

"Eureka," he said. "All clear behind?"

"Yes, sir."

Gramps backed out away from the bank, but he couldn't turn. "The blithering thing won't steer," he said. He got to the centre of the road, and the nose still pointed to the bank. Then Harry saw a steering arm trailing on the ground.

Gramps got out and inspected it himself. "That's cooked it," he said. "But we can't stay here. There's still a lot of fire about." Gramps thought it over, and Harry was glad that the problem wasn't his, that there was a man to deal with it.

"Well," said Gramps, "we'd better get the car off the road and walk. Though if we could run it'd be better. It's about a mile to Miltondale, I reckon. Maybe a mile and a bit. Blithering pest. Cars aren't what they used to be. Hit a train back in thirty-seven and drove away."

It looked so ugly outside that Pippa was glad to get back into the house. "I wish we had the wireless," she said. "I'd like to know what's going on."

Lorna shrugged. She wasn't quite awake. She was still in the old armchair.

"You haven't got a transistor, I suppose?" Pippa asked.

"No."

"The sky looks awful."

"How long have I been asleep?"

"About an hour, I suppose."

"Did you get your breakfast?"

"I had some cornflakes, thank you."

"You didn't cook anything?" Lorna said.

"The power's still off. I didn't like to light your wood stove. It's hot enough without that."

"What's the time?"

"Five to nine," said Pippa.

"Dark, isn't it?"

"I was telling you about that. The sky."

"Oh goodness," exclaimed Lorna. "Five to *nine!*"

"Yes?"

"The water! The carrots. The sprinklers haven't been shifted since five o'clock. They should have been shifted at eight. And the berries. All the berries we picked. They'll be out of the shade. The sun'll have moved round."

"There's not much sun, Lorna."

"Thank heaven for that." Lorna had reached the door. "I'd hate those berries to be spoilt. They were bad enough, and I'd hate them to get worse . . . . Maybe they'll be the last he'll ever pick."

"Don't say that."

Lorna looked different now. The desperation had gone. "I've got to face it, Pippa. They say it comes to everyone sooner or later."

"But just the same . . . ." Pippa thought it was bad to talk about it. "Where are you going?"

"To bring the berries up, of course, and to shift the sprinklers. I'd be letting him down if I didn't."

"I'll come with you."

They stepped outside and Lorna saw the sky, the light, the

smoke, the evidence of the continuing high wind. Hours had
passed since she had been aware of it. Perhaps the fire had been
dismissed from her reckoning from the time her father had
collapsed. There had been moments when the fact of it had cut
across events, there had been the continual harassment of its
influence on other people, but to Lorna it had been one part
only of a terrible experience, and not the dominating part.

Pippa sensed the sudden sharpening of Lorna's concern before
she expressed it. "Gosh," said Lorna, "someone's in trouble.
I've never seen anything like it. Have you?"

"No . . . ."

"I can see what you mean about a wireless. Gosh, I wonder
where it is? I wonder how far it's got? The boys lit *that?*"

"So they say."

"You tried the telephone again?"

"About half a dozen times. Dead as a doornail. I suppose
there's a tree down somewhere over the wires."

"Probably dozens of trees. I don't suppose Mr Robertson
called?"

"No. Should he have done? I think Stevie said he'd gone to
Miltondale and taken a lot of men with him. My dad was one
of them."

"He was bringing us a drum of fuel oil for the pump," said
Lorna. "I know we need it, too. We haven't got much."

They went down into the raspberries, with the dog for
company, out onto the open hillside. "That smoke's terrible,"
said Lorna. "You'd swear it was just over the hill."

That was what Pippa thought, too. But it couldn't have
been; it simply couldn't have been. Yet the sky was so full of
rubbish, of bits of bark and leaves and fern. It was all dead
stuff, but live pieces could have spread the fire, could have
carried it miles ahead of itself and started more fires. By now
there might be hundreds of fires impossible to contain, impossible
to control, with no one to fight them, no one to spot and report
them. The fire-fighters might even have given up and fled.
What could mere men do against fires that made smoke like
that?

An hour ago Pippa had thought it couldn't possibly get
worse, but it had. Now that they were away from the house,

the sound grew louder and they could smell sharper odours, of eucalyptus gases and the flaring juices of millions of growing things now spent; boiling clouds laden with the spoils of the forests were everywhere, for as far as the eye could see. Whatever were the fighters to do with it? How were they to put it out?

"I wish John were here," Lorna said breathlessly.

"And I wish my dad was, too."

"You know, Pippa, we might have to get out!"

"How?"

It was such a little word, but Pippa had never uttered anything more graphically profound.

Lorna shook her head. "Somehow," she said, without conviction.

"Yes, but where do we go?" Pippa with a trembling hand pointed into the south-east. "We can't go that way. It's all bush. The worst thing you can possibly do is get into the bush. That's what they've told us so often. And we can't go the other way, because that's where the fire is."

"You don't think it *could* happen, do you?"

Pippa bit her lip. "I don't know . . . . But I think I'll have to go home. There's Stevie. He'll be terrified. I thought he'd come here . . . . Oh, Lorna . . . ."

Pippa turned and ran. She could think of nothing except Stevie. And Julie. Julie was even closer to the fire than Stevie, Julie and Grandpa Tanner, that old, old man.

Peter looked back, and with a start saw Pippa.

Funny: he had supposed himself to be on his way home to look for her, but this had come too easily, too soon. He was on the point of darting for cover at the roadside—if he could have stirred himself sufficiently—when he saw that she was calling him. Though he couldn't hear her voice, he knew from the attitude of her head and body that she was crying out, appealing.

He stared at her hurrying and stumbling, and remembered his numbed vigil at the bottom of the carrot paddock. He had done that for her and she hadn't cared. She hadn't even known about it, or that he had worked out who had started the bushfires. She'd never understand what he had gone through, the loneliness, the misery, the awful tiredness, the grim battle to break through the invisible walls that had confined him. She would never know the effort it had cost him to walk out of the paddock. It had been terrible because it had been so strange. Nothing like it had ever happened to him before.

He didn't hide; he turned his back on her, suddenly angry, and tried to summon from himself what little dignity the morning had left him. He had no clear idea of what dignity was, except that the adult world he lived in placed a high value on it. It had something to do with tummy in, chest out, and chin up. Tears had no place in it; nor had tantrums or whining. Most of the time it was the exact opposite of how a boy felt, for when he felt mad he was supposed to look glad, and when he felt wildly happy he was supposed not to dance about and whoop. But it didn't seem to cover occasions like this.

He heard her voice: "Peter . . . ."

And he stopped at once. How could he walk away from her when she cried out to him? But his back was still turned to her, because he was afraid he was going to cry.

"Peter . . . ."

He tensed himself and felt her hand clutch at his shirt. "Oh, Peter, I'm so glad to see you."

She was in front of him now, and though he looked away from her, he knew she was flushed and frightened and too short of breath to pronounce her words properly. He hardened again, not expecting that he would, not knowing why he did. "You're only glad to see me when it suits you," he said. "I don't want to talk to you. I don't want to have anything to do with you."

She was trying to get her breath back. Perhaps she didn't really hear him. "Oh, Peter," she panted. "Help me."

"Why?" he said.

She clutched at his arm again. "We've got to hurry. Time's so short. There's so much to do." She made to go on up the hill, certain he would go with her, until she realized that she was dragging on him and that he was resisting her.

"Peter," she shrilled. "Come on. Quickly."

"I'm not going anywhere with you," he said.

She dropped her hand and stared at him. "What's the matter with you?"

"You know what's the matter. Or if you don't you've got the shortest memory I've ever heard of."

"We had a row," she said, astonished. "Are you holding that against me, at a time like this, after everything that's happened? You can see the sky, Peter. You can see what's going to happen, can't you? If we don't do something, people are going to get burnt to death."

"Don't talk stupid," he said.

"Stupid? What's stupid about it? Stevie's on his own. Julie's with Grandpa Tanner and they're on their own. And we're on our own. There's no one to help us. All the men have gone away. Even your Gramps has gone."

Peter's breath was coming faster and faster. His heartbeat was high in his throat.

From the sound he made Pippa guessed at once that he didn't know what she was talking about. Where on earth could he have been these past hours?

"You haven't been home?" she said, "Or anything?"

"Where's Gramps gone?"

"He's taken Mr George to hospital. Two of the boys went with him."

"Without me?" he exclaimed.

"Yes," she shouted. "Of course without you. What's that to get upset about? I thought you didn't want to go."

Now Peter wasn't sure what he wanted. "What's wrong with Mr George?" he said. Not that he was interested; the question was automatic; it came out of his confusion, out of his fright, for being abandoned by Gramps was altogether different from dodging him. To be denied an escape was different from not wishing to take it.

Pippa didn't answer his question. Her impatience with him flared again. His stupidity was too much to take. He *must* have known what had been going on.

"You're useless!" she shouted at him. And for the second time that morning she ran from him, hating him, wondering almost blankly how she had ever thought he was nice.

Peter watched her pass over the hump of the hill and out of sight, and felt utterly lost. Nothing else in heaven or on earth really mattered except that he had bungled his reconciliation with Pippa. She hadn't said the right words, nor had he. He had tried to be dignified instead of being just himself. With her passing from sight he was sure she had gone away for ever. It was an awful feeling, lonely and dark and empty. He wasn't even angry with her.

After a while he pushed one leg in front of the other and started plodding up the hill again. What had happened to this day was still a mystery to him. Pieces of it were plainer than others, though at first they came faintly, like tiny pinpoints of light a long way off, that had to grow brighter before he could see them clearly. Pippa may have been special once, but she wasn't special any more. She was just another girl, a playmate he had known when he was a little boy. Was that really one of the things that he could see? Was that as plain as the fact that Gramps had gone away without him, that Gramps for the first time ever had failed to enforce his will upon him? And that if Gramps had gone, Gran might be on her own and might need him, not as just a little boy to smother with love, but as a young man to protect her from danger? Unless Gran had gone with Gramps? Surely not.

Was he on his own, like Pippa and Lorna and Stevie and Grandpa Tanner and that unknown boy who had disappeared in the bush? Could he really be on his own, on his own two feet, in the face of this monstrous sky? Not dependent upon anyone? Not tied to anyone, even Pippa? Completely free? But to be a part of the inferno that he *knew* was about to burst from earth and sky?

Perhaps he was.

Peter smiled faintly, and there was strength in his body again, and the tears in his eyes were not those of a little boy.

11. Dead End

LORNA hurriedly pulled her trays of raspberries up to the front gate to get them out of the way. The Georges had a little rubber-tyred trolley for the purpose; John had made it from the wheels of an old baby-carriage. Though Lorna was sure the carrier from the jam factory wouldn't accept the berries, she left them in the usual place in the shade of a wattle-tree. Perhaps later in the day, she would try to pick more; in the cool of the evening, if the evening turned out to be cool, if the evening came at all.

Lorna was not wholly sure that there would be an evening, because minute by minute the day assumed aspects of still greater gloom and greater dread.

She ran after Blackie down into the carrot paddock. The sprinklers still were turning; wind-blown water still sprayed far and wide. But for how much longer would the engine continue to drive the pump? How much fuel was there? And she might need that water now, for other things: for damping down the house, for spraying the outbuildings, for those simple demands of survival that water alone could answer. If she had the strength to manhandle the heavy pipes . . . . But it couldn't happen. How could there be an end so terrible? Awful things like that might threaten, but they never came about. It always rained, or the wind changed fiercely and drove the fire back into burnt-out country, or hundreds of men with beaters and knapsack sprays and hoses arrived in the nick of time. Sometimes people said prayers and the prayers stopped it. Sometimes the fire came to a river and couldn't burn any farther. Sometimes it came up to the shores of a lake or a dam and that was the end of it. Sometimes it went out for no reason at all; just died down and went out. The life of a fire wasn't all that easy. From the moment it started everything in the world was against it. Even the wind wasn't always its friend; if the wind blew too hard it blew it out.

But Lorna knew that the special circumstances of this day were with the fire, not against it. There wouldn't be a wind-change because the wind was set; there wouldn't be rain because there was none within a thousand miles; there wouldn't be hundreds of men because a fire as vast as this monster that filled the sky was beyond the hand of man—the only men she could even hope to see would be exhausted men, beaten men, fleeing for their lives. But who would come this way, down this road, into a dead end? And prayers wouldn't stop it or they would have stopped it already; and rivers wouldn't stop it, and lakes wouldn't stop it, and dams wouldn't stop it, and it wouldn't die down and go out until there was nothing left to burn. Nothing could stop it until it reached the ocean, fifty, sixty miles away. The end of the world wasn't getting ready to happen; the end of her world was happening already.

She stood among the carrots, in the mud, with the cool water spraying her face, looking into the lowering sky, into the west and the north and the south, into an arc of smoke beyond measure, nothing but smoke and raining ash, and the leaves of ferns and trees and scrub and twigs and pieces of bark and lumps of resin as big as hen's eggs, falling. Many of them smoking. Many hitting the ground not dead. And thousands and thousands of birds in flocks flying east; hawks and eagles, crows and parrots, magpies and kookaburras, starlings and finches; birds free, flying overhead, and leaving her below. And somewhere a sound like a mighty wind but not the wind, somewhere a sound that she had heard about, that John had spoken of but had never heard himself for it did not belong to the fires that John knew; a sound that Grandpa Tanner had talked of once, a sound not unlike other sounds yet different from them all. Like a raging sea, but different. Like an earthquake, but different. Like an avalanche, but different.

What was the use of worrying about carrots? Or raspberries? Or outbuildings? Or the house? Or anything? There wasn't time. Or was there still?

She began to feel smaller. It was an awful feeling. It actually seemed to be happening. She turned up her hands and half-expected to see that they had become the hands of a baby. She cried a little and was surprised to hear that it was her own voice, not the cry of a baby.

"Please, God," she said, "send someone to me. I'm all on my own."

Except for Blackie. Blackie bounding towards her across the rows. Blackie barking in that way of his when he had found something, a wombat or a wallaby or an ant-eater or a snake.

Graham knew that something was wrong, but it was difficult to bring his senses to bear. He felt cramped, half-suffocated, and so, so tired. He didn't want to wake up. He wanted only to go on sleeping, to escape the feeling of despair that belonged to the conscious world. But the conscious world wouldn't let go of him; it dragged him out of sleep almost by the hair of his head. "Wake up," it said to him over and over again, and pricked at him with needles, hundreds of needles, right down one side of him.

He rolled over, suddenly grunting with pain, flinching from the agony of blood coursing through numbed veins.

He was awake, and the light in the gully was poor, so poor that he thought he had slept all day. The thought did not disturb him much; he still drew breath sharply to counter the pins and needles in his side; breath that tasted as bad as his mouth, breath that was not good, clean air. Gradually he realized that the gloom was not natural, not the gloom of evening. The face of his wrist-watch stopped swimming in front of his eyes and became clear. It was 9.28; 9.28 in the morning. It had to be, for by 9.28 at night there was no light at all.

Then he saw the dog.

The instant their eyes met the dog barked and the boy's heart leapt with fright. They weren't six feet apart. Then he saw the girl. She was kneeling beside him and he had not seen her sooner because he had rolled away from her. "Come on; wake up," she was saying. "Pull yourself together."

"I am awake," he said thickly, struggling to sit up, frightened of the dog, alarmed by the presence of the girl, oppressed by an awful feeling of failure that he was not for the moment fully able to understand.

"You'll have to get on your feet," she said, "if you don't want to be burnt to death. You'd have slept through it, you know. I *couldn't* wake you up."

He didn't understand.

"Get up," she said roughly. "Stand up!"

"My feet," he groaned.

"I can see them," she said. "What on earth have you been doing with them?"

"Oh, golly . . . . Go away. Leave me alone."

"Look here," said Lorna. "Do you want to stay alive or not?"

"I'm sick," sighed Graham. "You can see I'm sick. Leave me alone."

"So you do want to burn to death?"

"Eh? What are you talking about?"

"I'm talking about the bushfire. The fire you and your friends lit."

Graham suddenly felt cold; cold despite the awful heat; cold to his fingertips and the crown of his head; so cold inside that he didn't even have the will to deny what she said. Numbly he corrected her: "I lit it. They didn't."

"Graham's your name, isn't it?"

"Yes."

Lorna liked him for the pain in his dull eyes, for his dirty face, and for something else, she was not sure what.

"Graham," she said. "Let's be friends. I'll stick by you and you stick by me. The fire's coming. You've got to get up and walk. You've got to get up and help me. If you don't we'll probably both be burnt to death."

She was so matter-of-fact, so calm, so purposeful; it was plain common sense to do as she said. Graham took her hand and groaned on to his feet.

He held on to her hand and leant against her. "You're Lorna, aren't you?" he said.

"Yes."

"Is your dad all right?"

"I don't know."

"I'm sorry—for everything."

"That's all right. Wallace and Harry have gone with him, with Gramps Fairhall, to the hospital. They were going to ring me, but they can't, because the phone doesn't work. They should be back, but they're not."

"The fire?"

"I suppose so. It's terrible. Can you put your shoes on?"

"No."

"I'll take your pack. It'll make it easier for you."

"It's too heavy."

"It's too heavy for you, with your feet. Give it to me . . . . Hurry. Please hurry."

The men were to meet—perhaps by chance—on the last yards of the road above Miltondale, at the fringe of the State Forest, where the dark evergreens ended and bright deciduous trees and exotic shrubs and houses began. Where the forest had ended yesterday and the town had begun yesterday. Today the line was not drawn so sharply. Today there was a bond between them; of tongues of fire, of smoke, and of a common blackness.

Gramps Fairhall didn't know that the meeting was about to happen, nor did Pippa's father. The world could be a very small place in times of stress or danger.

Gramps and Wallace came round the last bend above the town carrying old man George between them. He was strapped to a car seat, inelegantly, grotesquely, and weighed about a ton. Every ounce of a ton. He was so, so heavy and their hands were so, so sore. Blistered. Even cut from the sharp edge to the seat. And their clothing was soaked with sweat, stuck to them, tugging and tweaking at them, and their bodies cried for relief, for water, for rest. Gramps was waiting for his heart to break or stop, but it pounded on, confusing his senses with its thunder.

Harry had given in. He had been sick so often that they had left him to follow when he could. He wasn't far behind, no more than a few hundred yards, and he had never felt sicker. He had swallowed too much smoke, and though he believed himself to be shocked less than the others, he was in fact shocked more. It hadn't taken long; only a few minutes; then it had come back over him like a gigantic wave or a gigantic noise. The rampaging fire-front, though behind him in time and space, enveloped him again in his mind. Then a second time and a third time. Then he had started screaming. Now he dragged his feet and hung his head; his arms and shoulders drooped. One moment he was feverishly hot, the next desperately cold. And he was dry. His thirst was raging, and he walked on only because he knew that if he didn't some tree still burning might fall upon him, some new blaze springing up might cut him off. The danger was no less real because he kept on the move; it only seemed so. If life for Harry had not held such promise, if he had not dreamt of someday being a man, he would have fallen to the road and not got up. Except that the road was hotter than the air. It was hotter than the sands of a desert. It was hot through the soles of his shoes.

Gramps and Wallace came slowly round the bend, and there below them were the outskirts of Miltondale, an odd blend of the living and the dead, veiled by smoke, in places still fiercely burning. Showers of sparks and billows of smoke driven by the wind into hillsides of ashes. Tall trees here and there unburnt, isolated garden copses unburnt, homes scorched but standing, elsewhere cracked chimneys rearing from twisted heaps of iron like blasted guns surrounded by bodies. And a smell. The curious smell of burnt things once used by men, the smell of burnt tables, burnt books, burnt beds, burnt armchairs, burnt bread. Things that burned with black smoke and green fire. Things that burned with white smoke and red fire. Things that smouldered. Things that exploded. Things that wouldn't burn but turned into powder. Things that cracked. Things that shattered. Things that melted. Things that vanished.

There were no people. The people had not come back. They were lucky to have had somewhere to go. There were no living animals or birds, no insects. There was a great sound of wind and burning, of things falling down; yet also a great silence, a great desolation.

They saw it but didn't see it. They were aware of it but could not take it in. They came down the hill towards it like actors on the wrong stage, and Pippa's father came up the hill on a bicycle. He didn't know whose bicycle it was; he didn't care. He hadn't ridden a bicycle in years and his calf muscles and thigh muscles were in torment. He had ridden it for three miles as fast as he could. He had begged for a car to drive him to Prescott, but cars were no longer going that way. They were heading in new directions now, south towards other townships, south along back roads and branch roads, and then west, swinging wide of the ranges towards the city, for Prescott was no longer the haven it had seemed to be.

He had hoped to borrow a car or take one, but the only cars left were cars burnt-out or cars that wouldn't go. He had found a motor cycle, but there hadn't been any petrol in it; he had found a motor scooter, but had been unable to start it. So he had taken a bicycle to ride ten and a half miles home; and having got it he had been afraid to put it down; afraid to dismount long enough to stop any passing vehicle on the road in case someone should take the bicycle from him. Cars heading out of the ranges would not turn back, anyway, and there were none at all heading in the direction he wished to take.

He saw Gramps Fairhall and Wallace coming round the curve down the hill towards him, but did not recognize his neighbour until the gap between them had closed to a few yards. By that time the steepness of the hill had beaten him and he was walking breathlessly beside the bicycle as fast as he possibly could, and Gramps and Wallace with their peculiar burden had drawn so close they looked like stretcher-bearers stumbling dazed from a battlefield.

Their eyes met, and in the manner of men under great strain, obsessed by their own concerns, they expressed no surprise and felt none. That they should meet in circumstances so out of the ordinary seemed the most natural thing in the world.

As far as Gramps was concerned there was no need even to stop. He was almost hypnotized. His body knew it had to keep plodding on until it reached the hospital or someone or something turned up to take over the responsibility. Buckingham with a bicycle was clearly not that person or object. If Buckingham had been driving a car it would have been different. Nor did Mr Buckingham see in Gramps Fairhall any relief for his own distress.

They passed each other by and Gramps said, "Where's Robertson's truck?"

"Heaven knows," said Pippa's father. "Police commandeered it and Robertson went with it."

Gramps grunted, as if he had known all along it would happen, and Pippa's father flushed again angrily at the recollection of it, for even then Bill Robertson and he had been on the way home, just the two of them. They hadn't got far when the police stopped them. It had been a raw scene. It was still hard to say who had been right—Bill Robertson or the police—but the police had won. Families as far away as Prescott were beyond reach, the police had said; there were other men's families who came first because they were immediately at hand. In the end an officer had pulled a gun. That had finished it, in a nasty way.

So Gramps and Mr Buckingham passed each other by before something stopped them; something that had nothing to do with politeness or neighbourliness; the faint and unwanted stirrings of something that might have been called duty.

Gramps said to Wallace, "Put him down," and Wallace responded automatically and sank panting onto the hot road beside the car seat, conscious of nothing but his own exhaustion. For the moment Gramps, too, felt like collapsing, but knew that if he did he'd probably never get up again. He swayed and wiped sweat from his eyes and felt light-headed and empty-shouldered. He pressed an arm against his thundering heart and heard Pippa's father say, "What are you doing without your car?"

Gramps had almost forgotten that he owned a car. "Back up the road somewhere. Broke a steering arm."

They exchanged looks, not really drawn to each other, even now. As a rule they put up with each other simply by avoiding each other as much as possible. "What's happened?" Mr Buckingham said.

"It's old man George," said Gramps. "Had a stroke, I think."

That meant nothing to Pippa's father. His mind couldn't reach beyond his own family and his futile attempts to reach them. "What's happened to Prescott, I mean?"

"Nothing that I know of."

"That's difficult to believe. They've cleared out. They've run for it!"

Gramps, also, was too fatigued to understand anything beyond his own problems: beyond the agony in his hands and body, and the compulsion to honour his obligation to old man George. "Prescott's all right," he said, "I just left it."

"This doesn't add up. I'd like to believe it, but how can I? Prescott was abandoned at nine o'clock."

Gramps, against his will, tried to summon out of a recent past not clearly remembered an appreciation of time. How long ago *had* he left Prescott? "Abandoned?" he said. "What for?"

"It's out of control. They can't stop it. They've given up trying."

"Prescott is?"

"The fire!"

Gramps slowly shook his head, still not understanding.

"They've pulled back into open country. They're letting most of the hills go. Better to let property go, they say, than life. They're lighting new fires in open country where they can control them. Lord, I ought to know. Burning breaks miles wide. It's the only way they'll ever stop it before it cleans up half the State."

Gramps continued to shake his head. "Abandoned?" he said. "They wouldn't abandon Prescott. You've got to be wrong, Buckingham." He began to feel towards this man an intense irritation.

"They can't fight it," said Mr Buckingham. "It's too big. It's leaping miles ahead of itself. You've lost track of time somewhere. Would I invent these things with a wife and children of my own in the middle of it?"

Gramps swayed and pressed his arm harder to his heart. Wallace looked up, red-eyed, still panting.

Pippa's father glanced at old man George. "Where are you taking him?"

"Hospital."

"They evacuated it two hours ago."

Slowly Gramps's legs gave way and he sat on the road, and his sigh meant more than words could ever express. "Oh, what a shame," he said. "What a downright shame . . . . And you're going home?"

Mr Buckingham nodded.

"You should never have left it."

"I know."

"Nor I."

Harry came round the curve, hunched and drooped, his eyes almost closed, arms flopping at his sides. He slouched past them and didn't see them, and Wallace struggled onto his feet and went after him to bring him back.

Gramps said, "We'll find a safe house and move in. Then we'll try to get help. I can't believe that everyone has gone."

He was talking to himself, for by then Pippa's father had gone and old man George was dead.

Pippa's mother, with Gran Fairhall and young Mrs Robertson, drove hard through the winding gully below Prescott.

They knew they had left their run late. They hadn't meant to; indeed, they had not suspected until nine o'clock that such a run would be necessary, for up till then Prescott had been a place that evacuees were coming to by the hundred, perhaps by the thousand, not a place that people were fleeing from. Before nine o'clock the three women had been caring for the frightened and the homeless and the weeping; now they were fugitives themselves.

In Prescott Mrs Buckingham had been caught in a snarl of traffic. Cars parked in the yard beside the Public Hall were all trying to get out at once. The drivers were not panicky so much as dismayed, and in their dismay and anxiety they misjudged distances. Three cars were locked bumper to bumper, another backed onto a tree stump and stuck. Mrs Buckingham could not move forward or backward or sideways. She had to wait behind them. Had to wait and wait. At last she had escaped into crowded Main Street and cut recklessly across its endless line of oncoming traffic to run free and fast down the side road towards home. By then it was after 9.20.

At 9.24 she came (for the first time) to the broken blackwood tree which blocked the way with a mass of foliage and fractured branches twenty feet high and which had borne power lines and telephone lines to the ground; the blackwood tree that no one had had time to clear away.

"I'll have to go the long way round, by the highway," said Mrs Buckingham.

"But how will you get through the town?" said Mrs Robertson. "The traffic's moving against you. There are *hundreds* of cars."

"I'll have to try."

"Wouldn't it be best to leave the car and walk or run?"

"It's more than a mile. Mrs Fairhall couldn't keep up with us."

"I couldn't. That's true."

"I'll hurry. I'll do it. Don't worry."

Mrs Buckingham turned the car and drove back to town. But she couldn't get through. Tears and threats, even gathering hysteria, were not enough to part the traffic. She put the car's nose out into the line of cars to try to break across to the left-hand side, but a man she knew ordered her back. He thrust his arm into the car and knocked the gears into neutral. "Go on back," he said. "Get back. Do you want to start a pile-up? What's wrong with you?"

"Our children are there," she cried. "Who's to warn them? Who's to get them out? It's a dead-end."

"Your children are not that way! They're *that* way!"

"There's a tree down. We can't get through."

"You'll never get through the other way; that's certain."

The character of the township had changed. There were drawn and haggard faces she had never seen before. Even the people she knew were different. They were there, passing across her consciousness; kind people with hard masks. Kind men who were acting rudely and roughly and others who were acting strangely. "There's a car," one yelled, pointing at her. "They've got room. Into it."

And a horde of people with armfuls of household pieces rushed towards her. She fumbled the car into reverse, and backed away, swerving wildly into the gutter. She wrenched the car out of the gutter and in tears drove back to the tree.

There they abandoned the car, scrambled down the bank and up again to skirt the fallen blackwood, and ran.

Time had ceased to mean anything. Time as an hour of the day was pointless. The only reality was the raging holocaust, heard but not seen, in the north and the west.

But Gran Fairhall couldn't run, and had no child to run for, anyway. Not even Peter. For Peter, she believed, was miles away, safe in his own home.

The others left her farther and farther behind.

And Pippa's mother could not run as fast as young Mrs Robertson.

The three women drew farther and farther apart in a frightful world where even adults feared to be alone if they thought of themselves.

Gran Fairhall had no one to think of but herself. If she had known how to handle a car she would have returned to it and driven away. But she couldn't. So she waddled on, puffing and blowing, in a sweat of fear, yet encouraged by the knowledge that at home she would find her identity. On the open road she was nothing, just a fat and nameless old woman that the overwhelming fire might leave unrecognizable, but at home she was Gran Fairhall, a woman of consequence, of property, and of dignity. If there had to be an end that was how and where she wanted it to be.

Stevie sat on the end of Julie's bed, cuddling the cat, interminably stroking it. Hundreds and hundreds of times he must have stroked it, sometimes singing to himself, sometimes quiet. The room had been bright enough when he went into it, but after a while he had drawn the blind to shut out the awful sky, to shut out the ash he could see falling down, to shut out the hot and horrid day that frightened him so, even to shut out the wind that he could see pulling at the trees, throwing twigs on to the roof of the house with a sharp clang of iron, and blustering angrily through the grass and the dust.

Stevie didn't like the fire any more. He didn't like his dad being away and his mum being away and Pippa being away.

It was horrible being alone, for even though he talked to the cat and sang to it, the cat didn't care a bit. Sometimes it purred; sometimes it couldn't even be bothered to do that. And the telephone that was supposed to ring didn't ring, though every minute he was sure it was going to; and no cars came down the hill, though dozens of times the wind sounded just like a car; and no one knocked on the door; nothing happened at all.

He wondered about "nothing". People were silly to say that nothing was nothing. It had to be something. Nothing was something that happened when nothing happened. Stevie didn't like nothing. It started buzzing in his head. It made a noise. It went round and round. It throbbed. It was a great big pain. Much worse than toothache; much worse than green plums. It even made him cry, it hurt so much.

The screen door crashed and Stevie leapt from Julie's bed and the cat skidded across the floor.

It was Pippa, Pippa floundering into the house all flushed and dishevelled and almost too breathless to speak.

"Pippa," shrieked Stevie.

She caught him on the run and hugged him and swayed with him. "I'm sorry," she panted. "I'm terribly sorry. Oh, Stevie, I'm so sorry." She pushed him away and looked at him. "You've been crying, too." She hugged him again until Stevie reckoned he had had enough of it. "Fair go," he said, wriggling free. "You're makin' a sissy out of me."

Stevie wasn't afraid any more. He even felt chirpy again. He bounced back like a rubber ball. "Where you been?" he said. "What'cha been doin'? Leavin' everythin' to me."

Pippa wasn't in the humour for that sort of thing, for she knew she had to get out on that dreadful hill again and start running again up to Grandpa Tanner's. "Stevie," she panted (she could *not* get her breath back). "I don't want to frighten you, but there's not much time . . . . I just can't imagine why Mum hasn't come home, or Dad . . . . Where *are* they?"

"Helpin' at the fire, of course," said Stevie.

She shook her head impatiently, breathlessly, almost tearfully. "I don't mean it that way . . . . Stevie, the fire's coming."

"Yeh?"

"Here. Here! Maybe in a few minutes. Maybe in a minute. I don't know."

"Here?" shrieked Stevie.

"Yes, yes, yes."

"Not right here? To our house?"

"That's what I'm telling you, Stevie. Haven't you seen it? Can't you see it for yourself? It's everywhere."

"But the fellas," said Stevie. "What about the fellas to put it out?"

"There *aren't* any fellows. There's no one. What have you done? Where have you put the water?"

"Eh?"

"The water! In the spouts. In the buckets. Over the walls. How much have you done?"

He didn't have to tell her. She could see from his face, from his shame, from his embarrassment. "You've done *nothing?*"

He shook his head.

"Oh, Stevie . . . . Our house. It's got to have water all round it and all over it, or it'll burn."

"But the fellas'll come, won't they?"

"We don't know. We can't be sure. Probably not. Grab a handful of rags and stuff them in the downpipes. You can climb up on to the roof over the lattice. Then I'll hand the buckets up to you. Be quick, Stevie."

"The carpets aren't in, or anythin'."

"The carpets don't matter."

"But we won't have time if it's comin' in a minute."

"Do as I tell you. Grab a handful of rags from the laundry. Anything will do. It doesn't matter what it is."

"So it's not comin' in a minute?"

"I don't know when it's coming," Pippa cried. "Just do as I say."

"All right," grumbled Stevie. "There's no need to do your block. I can't make girls out . . . ."

"You're wasting time!"

"One minute they're huggin' and kissin' you; the next—"

Pippa was almost frantic. She could have taken him by the shoulders and shaken the life out of him. She snatched two buckets from the kitchen floor where her father had left them, and rushed to the bathroom, plunged them into the bath, and reeled back down the passage, bumping into the walls, staggering from the weight, until she stumbled down the steps on to the path at the rear of the house. Stevie was there with an armful of what looked like perfectly good shirts and aprons. He hadn't made a move towards the roof. He seemed to be frozen.

"What's wrong with you now?" she yelled at him.

His reply was a plaintive whine. "Is it really comin' in a minute? Really and truly?"

"Oh, Stevie! Forget about it."

"Don't you think we'd better go somewhere safe, like down the creek or somewhere?"

She had to talk to him; there was no avoiding it. Even though the boiling sky seemed to be falling upon her, she had to still her own panic and appear to be sensible and level-headed. "All in good time. First things first, Stevie." (She sounded like a grown-up. She sounded so unreal she didn't even impress herself.) "When it's time to go we'll go."

"To the creek?"

"No. Not to the creek. I've heard that creeks boil."

"Boil?"

"And ponds and tanks and things like that; they boil, too. We've got to get out in the open away from trees and long grass and scrub. Right out in the open somewhere."

"Where?"

She didn't know. "We'll find somewhere."

"Like the potato paddock next to Grandpa Tanner's?"

"Yes," she said. "Like that."

"The fire won't burn there," he said. "The fire'll stop there. It won't come any farther, will it?"

"The fire won't stop," she said. "It's not that sort of fire. Now get up on that roof. And hurry. Because I've got to get up to Grandpa's. I've got to see about Julie." Pippa could feel her panic flooding back again; it was as violent as a storm or an explosion. *"Do as I say, Stevie!"*

He leapt for the lattice as if a whiplash had touched him. He scrambled up desperately, sobbing, frightened not so much of the fire as of Pippa: she was so nice one moment and so awful the next. As he crawled on to the edge of the roof he heard her again: "Wherever there's a pipe going down from the spout, jam some rags in it. Jam them in hard. We want the spouts to hold water, not leak out. While you're doing that I'll get more water."

She brought the water out in kerosene tins and saucepans and jugs and preserving-pans. She scarcely knew what she was doing, scarcely knew how she threw one leg in front of the other, for all that her legs wanted to do was to fold up. She wanted to see about Julie and Grandpa Tanner, but there was so much to do here first. That stupid boy; that stupid, stupid boy. All that time and nothing done. She was splashing water everywhere and slipping in it and trying to think of all the other things she was supposed to do. What *did* one do in a case like this? What was one supposed to do?

Were there things to be dragged out of the house? Were there business papers to be found? Were there special things, loved things, that had to be saved? If there were, what were they and where were they? And where was she supposed to put them? How could she protect them? Whatever they were. She couldn't isolate them, picture them, arrange them in order of value.

There was a block in her mind, a black emptiness. Her body rushed around like a frantic thing on one plane; the other plane, the one of logic and reason, was shut off. And she knew it was shut off. There was a door she couldn't beat down. She couldn't bring her body and mind together.

A mass of things to do, and she didn't know what they were. She had known once, but she couldn't remember now. A thousand things to do, and no time, no energy, no clear direction.

And every time she put a foot out of the door there was the smoke roaring over the top of the hill behind Grandpa Tanner's place; every time more and more roaring over that hill until it stopped her and held her fascinated, transfixed; roaring over all the hills, roaring everywhere, roaring through the great valley, obliterating it, roaring through the gully at the foot of the hill, roaring through the trees along the road, roaring across the garden.

It wasn't imagination. It wasn't the wind. It wasn't blood

or breath roaring in her own head. It was the smoke; it was the sky; it was the air so hot that plants were wilting and withering and birds in flight were dropping to the ground.

The roar was in the world around her, everywhere, in a world growing darker and thicker and denser; a world that was like an endless roll of thunder without lightning, without fire or flame, only noise, fearful noise, only smoke, only blackness that bore down with a weight that she could feel, with the brute force of a prodigious hand.

Then she saw Stevie. He came upon her suddenly; Stevie wide-eyed and deathly white, clinging to the edge of the roof line, peering down at her.

"Come down," she screamed. "Come down."

12. Men Stand Up and Fight

The end was coming. Grandpa Tanner could see it with his own eyes, could feel it in his heart. The end of eighty-seven years.

He sat beside the well, a little withered-up old man (whose legs were so bowed that Julie had sometimes thought of running between them). He looked terribly alone yet he was surrounded with friends: the ghosts of everyone he had ever loved.

He sat on the stump, the same stump where he had mused in the shade on hot days these many years past; and, probably for the last time, he was filling his charred and chewed old pipe. But there was no shade today, only the lowering gloom.

Above him was his garden, overgrown but fruitful still; Jonathan apples on the wilting trees and Santa Rosa plums and the great tossing chestnuts in flower, roses full-blown and foxgloves beaten down, and forget-me-nots thicker than weeds. And in the midst of the garden, tucked in, eighty or ninety yards away, his home, only its roof visible to him, with its inches of dust in the ceilings and its insatiable termites in the foundations and its old ornate thermometer at the kitchen door reading 116 degrees.

From time to time he called down the well: "Don't cry, little darling. Grandpa's here."

Now there was a vibration in the earth and a tempest in the heavens and Grandpa remembered the psalm that said, "The earth shook, and the heavens dropped at the presence of God." But this was not the presence of God; this was His absence. This was the work of man; what man had done and what man had not done.

Grandpa was not afraid; he was resigned. He had tendered his life's resignation when he lowered Julie and the Robertson baby into the well: very calmly, very deliberately, trying not to appear over-dramatic. He did not want to offend the ghosts gathered around. But it was not the sort of thing that one could do naturally. It was not like dropping a bucket down forty-four feet to water or stoking up the stove or tidying a bed; it was not like anything else he had ever done. Julie sobbing and strapped to a chair that turned slowly on the end of a clothes-line, Julie with toffees and chocolates and the conviction that Grandpa had somehow betrayed her; and the baby at the end of another line in a basket secured with safety-pins and woven leather shoelaces knotted end-to-end.

Grandpa was glad he had dug the well so long ago. He had often been glad before, in the drought and the dry, but never more glad than now. He was sorry, though, that he had to leave the house to burn, for he had built the house, too, with his own hands, with boards and planks and beams he had split from messmate logs with sledge-hammers and wedges and had shaved smooth with sharp axes. All the fussy bits that his wife Marjorie (who seemed very near to him now) had wanted; the extra rooms and sleep-outs as the extra children came along; the fernery, the pergolas, the playhouse now tumbledown. Soon it would all be gone as if it had never been. Perhaps in a year or two someone else would come along and build again: a stark, bare house with a flat roof and cement walls that would never look like anything but a stark, bare house with a flat roof and cement walls. He wished he could fight for his home as he had fought once before, but he was old and frail and his place was beside the well.

Grandpa also knew that Prescott had been left to burn. No one had told him; no one had come to warn him because Ash Road was out of sight and out of mind and all its other residents seemed to have vanished from the face of the earth. He knew that Prescott was empty or emptying fast because that had become the pattern. It was a new sort of pattern that he had followed with dismay from the radio until the power failed and the broadcasts mercifully were silenced.

The authorities directing the fight against the fire did not regard houses as homes, as things of the heart, but as expendable buildings that could be rebuilt after the fire from the proceeds of insurance claims. The world had become unwholesome and its values distorted, and Grandpa Tanner was glad that he was old enough to shake its dust from his feet without regret.

People were not standing up to fight as they used to do. They were not calling out of themselves the ultimate effort to survive with dignity as they used to do. They were running as they used not to do.

They were running now because at the start, before there were men enough to deploy against the fire, a few families had been ordered to run, and running had become contagious and an easy way out. As a short-term policy it was so much safer. The authorities could report with satisfaction: "The worst fire in living memory, but no casualties."

And when the fire gathered breadth and depth it had been easier to abandon empty houses to it than to face it and stop it, easier to speak of a master plan and hurriedly invent one than to admit mistakes and to stand up and fight. People, Grandpa knew, were too busy looking after themselves, their own skins and their own reputations, too busy inventing excuses. If they had gone in their hundreds, in their thousands, into those gullies behind Tinley—the gullies they had left to burn because the risk to life was too great—it would never have come to this blazing moment of truth. The sky would be blue not black, and Julie would be playing in the sunshine where she belonged, not sobbing at the end of a clothes-line forty-four feet down in the wet, cold earth.

"I'm staying with you," he called to her. "I'm here. When the fire's over they'll find Grandpa and then they'll find you. It might take time, little darling; the night might come and the sun might come up again, but they'll find you. Don't cry, or you won't hear them when they come. Shout out loud, won't you? When you hear them come, you sing out: 'Here I am, everybody. Down the well, safe and sound'."

God was the friend of little children; of that Grandpa was confident. But he dared not ask God to be the friend of an old, old man. Not today. Some things were reasonable and some things were not.

Young Mrs Robertson, on the way to Grandpa Tanner's, looked back and saw Pippa's mother as one might see from a great height a stricken person drowning in an ocean of mud.

Pippa's mother looked back and saw Gran Fairhall as one might see a distant climber ghosted by gases on the face of a mountainside, giddily, as if beyond the climber an active crater were blowing up.

Gran Fairhall looked back and saw the world melting, saw fire in the clouds hundreds of feet above the earth, fire like fluid hands and fingers, like the branches of trees shedding leaves, fire flashing on and off like the neon lights of a great city.

Peter walked into the house calling for his Gran.

"Say, Gran, I'm back. Gramps got the car ready yet?"

He hoped that the hearty tone of his voice would ward off the storm and suggest that his long absence was in order. It was a thin defence, but better than none.

"Are you there, Gran?"

The house was dark and quiet; quiet as a tomb might be while the earth above shook to the hooves of a stampede.

"Gran!"

He had expected to find something different; he was not sure what; but not this. Perhaps anger, perhaps tears, perhaps a house half-stripped of possessions or a house of fear, not an untouched house beset by reeling silence.

"Gran."

Then he saw the note on the table hurriedly scrawled by

Gramps. The room was not so dark that he couldn't read it:

> *Edna,*
>> *Off to Miltondale with old man George.*
>> *He's very ill. A stroke. Lorna needs you.*
>> *Ask the Buckinghams to drive you down.*
>> *Love, Percy.*

Peter frowned. There was no mention in it of himself, and how odd it was to see the Christian names, Edna and Percy, just as if Gramps and Gran were ordinary people. A note for Gran that she had not seen. Why?

Peter sat at the table. The breakfast things had not been cleared away. The electric clock over the kitchen bench had stopped hours ago, at 7.34. There were eggshells and bacon rinds, a carving-knife and an empty tea packet on the bench; a fallen dish-cloth on the floor; yesterday's date on the calendar still unturned. The calendar offended Peter's sense of history; the day had to be right; everything else could stay as it was. He adjusted the calendar and stared at the date: "January, Saturday 13." The devil's number. He returned to the table again.

He felt restless: thought of Pippa for a moment or two, then dismissed the thought; thought of Lorna George, but he scarcely knew the girl and she'd never bothered about him; thought of Pippa again. Blow Pippa!

The air about him was in a state of constant shock; it trembled, shuddered, cracked. Something was rattling; windows, perhaps, or crockery on shelves. How like the ocean it sounded; the roar of a huge sea crashing continually on a reef.

It was silly, really, doing nothing. He felt that he was cheating himself of something, but somehow he didn't want to step outside again, not yet. He wasn't quite ready to face it. To face what? Death? Gosh, no. Not that. But he knew there was something he had to face.

He didn't want to die. At least he didn't think so, but if he didn't go outside he wouldn't see it; he'd miss it. It'd come and go and it would be all over and he'd only see the ashes afterwards—the ashes of trees and sheds and houses. But if this house burnt while he was still inside it, what then? Perhaps he could run a bath and sit in it or soak some blankets in water and pull them over his head.

Peter was becoming more and more restless. There was something that had to be done, but it failed to present itself to him.

He stood up and twisted his hands together. He developed an irritating twitch in the corner of his left eye. Fresh streams of perspiration started from his armpits. But he wasn't frightened; he could say that to himself quite positively.

Perhaps he had better go outside; perhaps even down to the Georges', since Gran wasn't around to do it. But it was so far to the Georges'. Perhaps he ought to go down to the creek and swim in the dam or down into the pit under the house—the cellar, Gran called it—where the apples and the blackberry wine were kept.

He had been so sure that Gran would be at home. It made everything kind of awkward. It was hard making a decision like this on one's own. He didn't want to hide himself away from it as if he were scared of it, as if it were going to burn him up or something.

Pippa knew she had to get to Grandpa Tanner's, and then past Grandpa's to the potato paddock lying fallow. There was no other clear land except odd paddocks of a couple of acres. That meant she had to run towards the fire, not away from it. She knew that if people were to survive a fire like this one, they had to have space around them, open ground and open air, or lots of water. She did not reason this out: she knew it by instinct.

And people must not panic. If they panicked they had to be dealt with roughly. And she herself was so near to panic. Who was to deal roughly with her, except herself? She beat the palms of her hands against her brow, hurting herself.

She had to think. She had to break down the door that shut her body and her brain into separate compartments. She had to calm Stevie, had to calm herself. Their lives depended upon her.

"I want my teddy," Stevie said.

He had grown out of his teddy-bear years ago. "Not now, Stevie. Please, not now."

"Let me get my teddy. He'll burn all up."

These were the important things. These were the things she had to think of. "Quickly. Get him."

He ran into the house and she waited for him. The seconds seemed like hours. And in those seconds she saw fire in the smoke-swirling gully at the foot of the hill below her. Flames appeared in the trees, like unexpected lights at night; flames in the Buckinghams' own trees not three hundred yards from where she stood, the trees where she had searched that morning for Julie.

"Oh my goodness."

She wanted to break, but she held on. She wanted to scream, but she didn't. She held on and waited for Stevie and hurried him away from the door before he had a chance to look downhill. She bustled him, smothered his sight with her arms and her haste and her urging: "Now to Grandpa's. Quickly to Grandpa's. As fast as we can."

"I don't want to go that way," Stevie said.

She held his arm and dragged him to the gate. He seemed suddenly to be opposing her. His face looked different, and he drew his breath through his teeth.

"I won't go that way."

"You will!"

She didn't really want to go that way herself. _ stinct tempted her to run in the opposite direction, away from the fearsome sound, away from the roaring smoke clouds billowing over the hills, away from the heat that came like a mighty wind.

He fought against her and tried to break her grip. She didn't know where her strength came from, but her grip on his arm was brutal.

"You're hurting!"

She dragged him after her. Grandpa's gate looked a mile away.

"No, no, no," he screeched and kicked at her ankles, and she lost him. He broke free and ran from her.

"Stevie! Come back! You mustn't run that way! *Come. back!*"

But he fled downhill, weeping; and how could the legs of a little boy run faster than a fire that might be about to burst above him?

Pippa went after him, at first because she had to, then because she couldn't stop herself. Her weak-kneed stride settled naturally into the downhill grade. She reached out her hand to grab Stevie, but he was always a little ahead, screaming, "No, no, no." Then, when she could have reached and grabbed him, fear held back her hand: fear of turning again to face the uphill grade. It was so much easier to run down than up, to turn one's back than to present one's face.

It was too late for Grandpa; too late for Julie.

"Oh, Julie," she sobbed, despising herself as she ran on downhill with her arm outstretched to grab Stevie, to stop him, yet never quite reaching him.

They would end up at the Georges', under the sprinklers, but only if they ran faster than the fire.

13. The Moment of Truth

PETER opened the front door—as if to step outside to take a breath of air—and walked along the veranda. He had started coughing spasmodically and his twitching left eye was watering. He wasn't crying, really; it was the smoke. At times visibility was not much more than fifty yards; at others it opened up.

Peter didn't know why he walked along the veranda. Possibly it was because of what he had to do. Something said to him: "Get outside and walk along the veranda." So he did. It was as if Gran had said it, or Gramps. He saw, then, the fire burning in grass against the fence. It was not a very big fire; it looked almost neat and tidy, like a fire purposely lit to clear the fence line. Yet it was a bigger fire than Peter could have stamped out with his feet or extinguished with a bucket of water. He was not sure what he should do about it. He didn't particularly want to do anything except watch it. Perhaps there were others?

There were, too. Curious little fires. Dozens of them. There were tails and puffs of smoke up and down the road, across the paddocks, even in the garden. There were hundreds of little fires falling out of the sky, riding along on the wind like nightmarish birds, some coming straight down and very fast, others whirling round and round, others passing high above the trees.

Against a clear blue sky and green grass the sight would have taken his breath away; now it was gruesome and ugly. There seemed to be lightning flashes and thunder claps rolling one into the other to form an almost continuous explosion; and outside the thunder claps a vibrating roar and gusts of wind like steam under pressure buffeting every living thing from all directions. Trees and plants were bowing and bending back and forth, to left and to right, in complete disorder, as if suffocating, as if throwing themselves about in search of cool, fresh air. There were spirals of wind laden with leaves and dust, and the gate, off its latch, banged open and shut. And there were other sounds: giant trees along the roadside groaning mightily, and other living things that Peter could not see, screaming.

This was not how he had imagined it would be. He had imagined trees burning like candles, silently; forests of beautiful candles, and people running with their arms in the air like supplicants praying. Something like Christmas in a cathedral; reverent, majestic, awe-inspiring. Not brutish like this.

Nor lonely like this.

No one to talk to. No one to watch running by with their arms in the air. No one to share it with, not even Pippa, because Pippa wasn't special any more.

Peter felt confused and disappointed and incomplete. Simply to occupy himself, he walked off into the garden, into the stinging spray of grit and dust and leaves and ash, first to let the fowls out of the hen house, then to stamp on all the fires that were small enough to stamp on. Those that were too big he didn't bother about. He moved from fire to fire, his eyes smarting painfully and his breath coming with labour. A single cinder like a branding-iron dropped out of the sky and burnt through the shoulder of his shirt. It hurt terribly, and he had to tear the shirt off to get rid of it.

After that he went back to the veranda and stood with a hand pressed to his shoulder, watching the fires multiply. Slowly his lips drew back and his teeth began to show. He was seeing things very clearly, too clearly. He was not dazed or dulled or paralysed, but he still felt incomplete, desperately incomplete, even after the last shades of the fire he had imagined fell away.

A fire that burned minutes before it arrived was quite beyond imagination. He was certain that some fires were starting where cinders had not dropped, because now the house was burning also, inside.

Grandpa Tanner put his pipe down on his tree stump, and poured a bucket of water over himself, and called down the well, "I'm still here, little darling. Grandpa's going to make it dark now. And remember what Grandpa said. When you hear them come shout out loud, as loud as you can, 'Here I am, everybody. Down the well, safe and sound'." With difficulty, for the wind was troublesome, he slid two sheets of corrugated iron across the top of the well, and weighted them down with rocks, and painted on the iron with black enamel: *Children Here*.

Then he curled up on the leeward side of the stump, drew a wet woollen blanket over himself, and bit very hard on the stem of his pipe.

When Pippa's mother stumbled through Grandpa Tanner's gate fires were burning in the long grass near the house and a clump of young gum-trees was weirdly flaring as if the leaves were formed wholly of gases. But of eerie destruction she was not aware; she saw only young Mrs Robertson returning from the house, reeling rather than running, almost as if swimming in a current of unstable heading. They closed into each other's arms and held on.

"They're not here."

"Has he left a note?"

"Nothing."

They clung to each other, fighting for breath, producing their voices out of a groaning emptiness.

"Better try my place."

"I couldn't run."

"You'll have to."

They got back onto the road.

"He couldn't have got far. He's so frail."

"Perhaps the police?"

"Yes, yes."

"The children are all right."

"Of course they are."

"We'll be safer at my place. The lawns are cut. The garden's clean."

They tried to run again. Air burned into them like fire. Their lungs were like fire. Their throats were like fire. And Peter saw them coming, reeling, their arms at their sides, not waving over their heads. They didn't seem to see him until they were almost upon him.

"Gran's house is on fire," he said.

"Peter!"

"Gran's house."

Pippa's mother was almost past speech, almost fainting. "Peter, Peter. What are you doing?"

"Gran's house is on fire."

"The children? Why aren't you with them? Didn't you go with them?"

"Go where?"

"Haven't they gone?"

"Gone where? Pippa went home. Where's my Gran?"

"Pippa went home?"

"Where's my Gran? Her house is burning down."

"Oh, the children."

"Where's my Gran?"

"Coming." Mrs Buckingham waved an arm at the long hill and said, "You stay with us."

"My Gran is back there?"

But the women were not there to answer him. They were running away from him.

"My Gran is back there?"

He couldn't see her. She wasn't coming at all.

"Back there?" Peter cried. "Not back there!"

The women had told him to stay with them, but a single pace after them was all he could take.

"I'm coming, Gran," he said, and went. This was what he had had to do.

14. The Crucible

AT the house the women found the buckets of water, the kerosene tins, the preserving-pans, the jugs, all the utensils that Pippa had filled with water; and the fire in the gully at the bottom of the hill, now raging, and more fires over near the eastern boundary fence, and others up the hill towards Grandpa Tanner's. Smoke even seemed to be coming out of the ground, out of fissures or cracks. There was smoke even where vegetables were green.

Pippa's mother croaked the names of her children—if they had been there they probably would not have heard—and went down on her knees near the back step where the water was spilt and wept without tears, without sound. For the moment, all that had sustained her had gone.

Young Mrs Robertson floundered past her into the house, calling for her baby. She found her way back to the kitchen and fastened her fingers like talons to the frame of the door, drawing deep breaths of heat and smoke and ever-sharpening vapours. She was a pretty young woman usually, poised and well-groomed. All that had gone now; all her looks, all her grooming, all her poise. "Not here," she said, looking down through the wire screen at the woman kneeling weakly on the ground.

"Just gone," said Pippa's mother, "only moments ago."

"But where?"

"God be with them."

"The boy hasn't come."

"What boy?"

Peter ran hard. Like most thin people, light-limbed and wiry, he was very fast on his feet. He had often surprised people by his speed, even his house master at school (his house master, however, had done nothing about it, because Peter Fairhall was a difficult child, a loner, usually stuck in a corner somewhere with a book).

Peter ran now as he had never run, with elation. He knew without being able to frame the words, that he was running into manhood and leaving childhood behind. He hated childhood. He ran away from it with joy. He was ready to prove himself a man; ready to be baptized a man with fire, whether he survived the ordeal or died from it. He didn't care about the cost, except that his Gran should live to know—and that everyone should know—that her life had been given back to her by him.

He ran, not blindly but with difficulty, into the face of fierce heat, expecting his Gran to appear, wraithlike, out of the smoke. She didn't. He drew nearer and nearer to the tempestuous crest of the long hill, the blind crest that marked so distinctly the division between the little world where the Fairhalls and the Buckinghams and the others lived, and the beginning of the great world beyond. But still she did not appear.

He came to the crest, and a spectacle of outrageous splendour stormed and funnelled and sheeted. The fire was a mile away, perhaps only half-a-mile, he did not know; except that the dam had not stopped it, that in the midst of it the dam bubbled and steamed unseen, and the Robertsons' blew up unseen, and the Collins', unseen, shrivelled into the earth.

It came upon his vision as something living and evil, shapeless and formless, constantly changing, huge beyond comprehension: an insane creature of immense greed consuming everything around it whether the taste pleased it or revolted it, rejecting what it did not care for only after it had mauled and

savaged it, then pitching it aside or spitting it into the heavens.
The heavens shrieked with the indigestible things that the fire
hurled from its mouth, spraying after them a froth of fury,
flaying them with its ten thousand tongues, whipping before it
the terror-stricken survivors of the deep green forest: screaming
rabbits and wallabies, bush rats and mice, milch goats and cows,
dogs and cats, children's ponies and wombats as fat as pigs,
lizards and snakes, and creeping and crawling and flying things.
But not Gran Fairhall.

Lorna and Graham stood side by side in the mud of the carrot
paddock, holding hands. It seemed the most natural thing in
the world to do. They seemed to have known each other all
their lives; and they knew that they would continue to know
each other for the rest of their lives, whether they lived scores of
years or only a few fiery seconds.

They stood saturated in the mud within the arc of the
sprinklers from the farm buildings and the tall trees, watching
fires appear mysteriously in the encircling forest, watching
flames start up suddenly and gather in the gloom.

Then, little by little, in spasms, the sprinklers began to fail.
Those higher up the hill ceasing before those lower down, they
drooped and tiredly retracted, as if the nozzles of the sprays had
wearied of giving out and wished now to take back.

"What's wrong?"

"Perhaps it's for the best," Lorna said. "We would have
scalded to death if the creek had boiled." But she thought:
"Dad has done it again. Run out of fuel."

The women put plugs in the wash basin, the sink and the
laundry troughs and turned on all the taps. Before they had
finished, the water had stopped running. The tanks were empty.

They dragged the carpets into the open away from the house,
down to the wet ground at the foot of the path where the
household drains seeped into the earth and where the overflow
from the bath had earlier found its way. The cord carpet from
the hall, crisp and dry; the mat from Stevie's room, and the
deep rug from Pippa's room, still limp and damp; frantically
they placed them one above the other, drenching them with

water from buckets and kerosene tins, preserving-pans and jugs, from all the utensils that Pippa had filled. Then they crawled underneath them.

Peter ran on as if drunk, pushed by fierce winds that now roared not over or through the monstrous thing that filled the valley, but towards it; winds sucked in from cooler places that fed smoke and dust and debris in gigantic clouds, in gigantic whorls, back into the furnace; winds that deflected the searing heat of the advancing furnace, and deflected smoke and vapours and dust and rubbish straight up to the sky. Cool air and boiling air met thunderously, explosively, and ahead of it Peter found his Gran at the roadside.

Though she had fallen heavily she felt no pain. She was past feeling, past caring; mercifully dazed and stupefied.

"I'm here, Gran," Peter called.

She gave no response.

"Gran! You must get up!"

She didn't move.

"Gran," he roared. "Get up!"

She looked at him vaguely as if confronted by a stranger, and deliberately, positively, he slapped her face. He shocked himself, for the impact stung through his hand and through his head. It sharpened her and it sharpened him. "Get up," he screamed.

And she got up, heaving her bulk onto her feet, tottering, until he slapped her again. "Move," he screamed. "Move yourself," and grabbed her arm and dragged, and she came after him like a reluctant beast yoked to a heavy load.

He fought off the road, through the ditch, heaving and pulling her into the sharp scrub, the scrub like needles—the acacias, the sword grass, the dogwood, the brambles, the burrs —and tumbled her through the wire fence into the potato paddock. She collapsed into a heap again, limp and quivering, and he slapped her back onto her feet with ferocious determination, screaming at her, "You will not die. You will not." He propelled her across the face of the hill, across the line of the furrows, driving her like a broken-down bullock, until a huge blast of incredible heat seared out of the north across the open ground. He had an instant's warning, a reflex, and threw her down with paroxysm of strength, and dropped beside her, and the blast went over him like raw fire.

If Peter had still been a boy of only thirteen years, he would have cried then from the pain through his thin singlet and from the bitter, bitter disappointment. They were going to die here; they were never going to rise again because the abhorrent thing raging and writhing across the valley was upon them. But he didn't cry, didn't have time to cry, because suddenly, blasting back out of the south, came cooler winds: winds still of great heat, but cooler, roaring back in again with dust and debris in stinging clouds.

He found his feet again, almost blinded. The face of the hill was still there, like an ocean rock swept by spume, or a desert prominence lashed by sand, or metal liquifying in a crucible. The face of the hill was there, but it was no longer motionless, no longer immovable. It seemed to slip and slide, shivering like an agitated fluid, heaving. It would not remain fixed, and Peter dropped again, felled by heat and sound and dizziness.

It wasn't the hill; it was in his head, in his body, in his blood.

He got up again, and his grandmother rose like a drugged creature of low intelligence responding to unwanted orders, and together they moved again, wading rather than running, as if the earth had turned to mud and sought to hold them fast; on, as in a dream, across the curiously contoured brow of the hill with the heavens above them like a breaking wave: a breaker of blackness and brilliance and satanic grandeur, of scarlet and gold and purple, blue and orange, brown and black, turbulence and oiliness and gas: a breaker perpetually at the point of breaking, curved, crested, like a flare from the face of the sun.

Peter fell and the earth fell with him, shot from under his feet. He skidded and tumbled, rolled in a shower of dirt and pebbles, over and over, steeply down the face of the rocky subsidence; his Gran somewhere near him, rolling and tumbling through grass and burns and scrub, her cries unheard, her hurts unfelt.

They tumbled into the pool among the basalt boulders, into the welling spring that was the source of the creek below Grandpa Tanner's and the Buckinghams'.

The water was shockingly cold.

With them in the water were creatures of the forest, things that crept and crawled, even snakes.

Stevie staggered across the rows of carrots towards Lorna and Graham, groaning for breath. His hair was singed, his eyebrows were singed, and there were holes burnt in his shirt, for the bush along the roadside near the George's gateway had been burning; cyprus trees along the path to the house had been burning; even the trays of raspberries had been burning.

But Pippa stopped running.

For a moment she couldn't understand it; couldn't understand why the will to move suddenly left her, why her knees gave way, finally and absolutely, and carried her slowly, buckling, almost with gratitude, to the earth.

She knelt as if crawling, her trembling hands planted squarely across the lines of withered seedlings. Then her wrists gave way and she leant on her elbows, and her shoulders gave way and, totally exhausted, she flattened on the hot red ground. She couldn't get up. She'd never get up. Never, never had she known a tiredness like it.

But there was a new sound in the heavens, a sighing, as if a giant as large as the earth had expelled the last breath from its lungs. She felt its breath pass over her. Every living and growing thing bent to it, shuddering as it passed. And there was light of another kind, and sound of another kind, and in the sky a collision, a convulsion, a conflict of giants.

Lorna, too, stopped running. She was running uphill towards Stevie and Stevie was running downhill towards her. She was saying some sort of prayer when she stopped running and the prayer died in her, forgotten, for she saw that collision in the sky.

Pippa's mother and young Mrs Robertson, hiding under the carpets, could not see it; they heard it.

Peter saw it, for it happened above him, to his left and his right, all around him, a flash of incredibly brilliant light from sky to earth or earth to sky, and an explosion that stunned him, numbed him, almost crushed him.

Then it fell like huge hot drops of metal, heavy like the sap of trees or globules of honey. It was even the colour of honey, sometimes burnt honey, sometimes golden.

The juices of the forest so greedily sucked up the heady juices of gum and pine and acacia, and the wind-blown salts of the earth and the sweat of men and the blood of beasts and the steam of ditches and ponds and creeks and rivers and reservoirs, of tanks and hoses, of irrigated fields and mud puddles, seemed to have become too heavy a load for the sated heavens to bear, and having weakened, having allowed the first drops to fall, they seemed to be spilling the lot over.

Black rain, red rain, golden rain, steaming rain, crashed onto the earth, and the sound was real thunder and the jagged light was real lightning and the giants of north wind and south wind, of the inferno and of the breadth of the wide cool sea, were locked in conflict.

Peter and Gran Fairhall dragged themselves from the spring, away from the snakes and the other swimming creatures, and the mammoth flare in the sky had dissolved, had vanished, had become a tempestuous brown fog.

Gran, confused but revived, awfully battered but conscious, wrapped her huge fleshy arms about her grandson, as she was often apt to do, and hugged him tight. For years Peter had detested it, had endured it with a set face and a pounding heart; but that had been the way of a boy, not the way of a man. Gran even sensed the difference herself and faintly heard his voice: "It's all right, Gran. Everything's all right now."

Pippa felt it beating on to her body. At first it came hot like her morning shower and she thought it was fire; but it did not consume her; it grew cooler; and cooler still.

She was wet now, and there was the smell of wet earth in her nostrils, the smell of wet smoke, the smell of wet dust sprayed with raindrops. She raised herself on her hands and knees, and cried and cried.

Stevie stumbled past Lorna, not seeing her, missing her by yards, on and down the hill until he knew that something had changed; that the open hillside was ringed not only by flames but also by smoke of a new kind, white smoke as clean as clouds, like masses of clouds rolling along the ground; that the wind was not hot at his back but cold at his face; and that water, not fiery ash, was pouring from the sky.

Stevie sighed; he sighed all over, from the pores of his skin and the hairs of his head. Fears and pains that were like hoops of steel about his chest unwound, dissolved. Relief took their place, relief like a soft bed or cooling oils. Relief and something else: wonderment that it was all over, that it ever happened, and that he still held his teddy-bear by one limp paw. He looked at it, almost with shame. "Gee whiz," he said, and furtively dropped it and walked away from it and hoped that no one saw.

Lorna saw, but Stevie's secret was safe with her. Rain streamed from her hair and into her eyes and from the tip of her nose. Her clothes clung to her as if she had swum through a stream fully dressed. She felt like a woman, standing there, proud in a way, dignified in a way, ready for whatever life was going to do to her. No longer lost. No longer frightened. Thankful that what her father had built had not been wholly destroyed. There was enough left to carry on, with him or without him. She couldn't have wept like Pippa even if she had tried.

Graham saw her standing there, separated from him by rain and smoke and the private thoughts that froze her like a statue. He was afraid of anything that might cut her off from him, even her thoughts. He didn't know her, not really, except that when she was near him she made him feel equal to anything, even to a public confession of what he had done, even to a determination to seek out a policeman at the earliest possible moment. She had said: "I think you've got to face it, Graham, and the sooner you face it, the sooner it's going to be over. It will be so much simpler than running away. And you didn't do it on purpose, did you? It really was an accident."

She made him feel complete as he had never felt before. She filled a gap in him that Wallace and Harry had never been able to fill, because to Wallace and Harry he had attached himself. He had never felt he really belonged.

Was this the feeling that grown-up people meant when they talked of love? Perhaps it was, because when she turned to him again he limped towards her as quickly as he could go, already feeling strong again.

Grandpa Tanner looked out, almost in bewilderment, from

beneath his blanket. Red fire was changing into hissing steam and frantic billows of smoke. The last flames around him were leaping and cracking like angry whips, and, having cracked, they disappeared eerily like genii in an instant.

He was not to die, not yet.

It was a disappointment.

He was alone again; the ghosts had gone. They had come so close, and then had gone away. He had no need of them now, for he was still an old man with an old house; he still had a roof for his head. No stranger would be building a stark, bare house with a flat roof and cement walls; not yet.

Grandpa had not meant the prayer for himself. Surely he had made it clear that it was for Julie and the Robertson baby and for little children everywhere.

But God had sent the rain. Of course He often did, though not always. He had built that provision into the plan of nature. Great fires drew to themselves great winds, opposing winds, and great rains. But not always. Just sometimes. Perhaps when men forgot themselves and prayed for little children; not when they shook their fists in fury and defiance.

Grandpa laid his blanket aside. It was ruined. There were dozens of tiny scorch marks on it and several large burns. It had been a good blanket. It was a shame.

Then he pushed the stones away from the sheets of iron with his foot, and a shrill but hollow wail rang from the depths: "Here I am, everybody. Down the well. Safe and sound."

R3